Wrong Parting

Tania Brassey

ISBN: 978-969-609-270-4

—

"Be not inhospitable to strangers lest they be angels in disguise"

George Whitman

Editorial team: Paris Norriss
Cover Design: Lynn Davies

CONTENTS

ACKNOWLEDGEMENTS

O Hail to Rowan Fortune at Cinnamon Publishing for weaving these pieces into a bewitching sarong!

For years of encouragement, thank you Barrow Poets, William & Susan Bealby-Wright.

To Molly, my mother, for being on these missions improbable.

PARADISE ROAD 1

I'm so carried away ogling the liner docked inside Fort Harbour, I don't realise Selma and Mignon are no longer strolling ahead. The pavements are awash with gaggles of sun-frocked tourists but my mother has vanished. The Eiffel Tower Cafe has its illuminated sign on. It's one place that her new best friend deems clean enough to patronise.

Panicking, I tear up to its first-floor entrance. To my relief, I can see Mignon's large frame, dwarfing the manager who is leading them to the terrace where extra seating is laid on for the overflow of visitors. Mignon and Selma are deep in conversation and have not noticed my absence. Phew!

I allow them time to settle. Let my breath even out, comb fingers through my hair.
'There you are!' Mignon snaps. 'So why don't you... cool off outside? They'll take forever with …'

In a theatrical whisper, 'We can tell hoi polloi by the cheap handbags, can't we. All fakes from China, what else?'

Selma winces. I share her embarrassment and step onto the terrace where sun umbrellas cast a welcome shade. My mother fawns on her friend because she's rich. I've hated Mignon since coming to Casa Bianca. Selma had a hitch with our arrangements for the school holidays so she called it 'a minor miracle' when Mignon offered us her place. Miracle sure! Since this haughty Eurasian witch is not keen on children.

Before we set off from her Art Deco villa enclosed by 11 acres of flamboyant, ironwood and hamilla, I picked my time to ask Selma a question burning on my tongue. We had followed Mignon for her to back the Chevrolet out of the garage. With the motor turning there wasn't a chance Mignon—already inside—could hear a thing I say.

'When can we go home?' I keep all expression off my face.

'What do you mean "go home?" Home - where?'

Mignon settles into her seat taking off court shoes, putting on driving flatties, checks the mirror, starts to reverse.

'I mean, when can we go - from here?' my voice barely audible 'How long are we staying at Casa Bianca?'

Selma is pinched and frayed as if she might like to know the answer herself. Mignon reverses smoothly. If Selma has an answer for me, she doesn't have time to deliver it. We climb in, Selma in the front. Me behind. As we reach the end of the drive at the half open gate, Mignon turns to my mother.

'You can't think of going until you've met this clever creature of mine – Queenie?'

Selma is startled; she stares straight ahead so her eyes don't betray her but I notice she swallows hard.

'-the one who reads the Tarot cards?'

'Aaah, yes.' My mother is reviving from the surprise. 'Must do that…'

'She is a gem!'

My jaw must be in my lap. How could the witch guess what I had just said?

'She is priceless! The things she can tell you -' Her eyes are on the road but her jowls work overtime; they do when she is cooking up mischief.

By the time we reach the seafront in Colombo, Mignon has whipped Selma into a froth about what Queenie has foretold and come to pass. As we turn at the sandstone replica of the Pantheon—our old Houses of Parliament—my mother is agog to meet Queenie. The advantage of being on this roof terrace is that it raises you high as the decks of the passenger liner perched snug against the quay. This dazzling liner is so close it blocks my view of Colombo Harbour. It's the first time I have seen a ship this close. I have watched them on the horizon, appearing like toys when we strolled to the seafront in the evenings—*before* Casa Bianca.

Mostly, it was cargo ships but one cruise liner was crisp and spotless with hundreds of twinkling lights looking like it was cut-out of cardboard. Mignon's mansion is like that: white, starchy, isolated amidst its sea of trees moving as green waves; dozens of small glass windows meant for a cooler climate. The square proportions of the house are like decks stacked together.

The brass is ship-shape, gleaming chocolate floors dotted with antique rugs, and Mignon as the Purser barking orders at her crew of navvies who would desert ship, given the chance.

I pick my way full circle round the terrace and return to the other side of a potted palm obscuring the table where the two are *churu-churufying*. Mignon will skin me alive if she catches me this close; I pray the palm blocks me from her view.

'This is your best chance Selma…'

Selma makes a noise between a snivel and a hiccup.

'You're the only person the suspicious beggar trusts. Don't waste the opportunity. The healthy Up-Country air is what his lungs need…he can listen to chamber music till his ears rot and fall off.' Her tone is iron-clad.

'… nowhere else has that level of nursing staff, no…'

'You'll visit him every now and then…'

'No darling!' my mother yelps as if she's been kicked. 'That I can't promise -'

'Only now and then?'

'A bare-faced lie? My God!'

Mignon's face changes colour 'You still go Up-Country for The Races, don't you?'

'Not anymore—all long finished with...'

'He doesn't need to know that…' her face, plastered in pancake make-up, quivers in annoyance.

My mother gets out her compact and presses her lips. The waiter brings the drinks but Mignon jowls won't stop working, sharpening her teeth to bite Selma's nose off.

'We're not getting younger, Mrs Hazell,' she coaxes 'You're wise to take the nest-egg and escape this miserable hell-hole. Letting that brother hoodwink you out of your small inheritance was misfortune, right? Then the other bugger saddles you with a bit of baggage that won't match the rest... hmm! Less said the better...'

Selma glares at the tanned naval officers in their tropical Whites ordering another round, attempting their few words of tourist Sinhala with the barman. She wishes she were among them, I can tell.

'Since you know what it's like in Europe, how can you stand this penny-pinching? Nobody gives a red cent to educate your cafe-au-lait...'

'I won't let you down.' Selma has something stuck in her throat.

Mignon shuffles in her purse so I must move or miss my drink.

'... the ideal person to persuade him. Just don't get cold feet dear.'

I pick up my glass and realise it's not a drink, its ice cream melting nicely. Yah!

I can have ten of these in a row and I'll never get cold feet.

'I'm thinking of... Australia' my mother says solemnly.

'You're wha-at?'

'Er... living there...? after it's done and dusted'

'Bah!' she sounds like the braying of a jungle crow.

'Why, dear?'

'Well, *you* would not meet opposition, having a British mother.' She pulls out a spiky hair ornament to scratch her scalp under the back-combed chestnut chignon 'don't you think they have enough er… indigenous types? The Australians allow more Sambo's in? Tall order!'

I lap up my Neapolitan ice cream, saving the brown quarter, as always, for last. It tastes better than the pink or the yellow.

Maybe Mignon feels she's been too severe. She drags Selma to Inner Beauty: the manageress does facials for Madame and has to put up with her insulting the manicurists who can't answer back. After a hairdo, my mother will be malleable for a visit to Mignon's Jesuit. Selma remains silent in the car. Before we reach the redbrick wall separating Casa Bianca from the rest of the world, she announces a headache from baking under the hooded hairdryer.

Yippie! I won't have to wait for a sticky hour in the car while the mossies swarm. Boss Woman subjects me to this during their sessions at the monastery. I'm not allowed to stroll in their lovely shady garden. Yet after a short siesta, Selma recovers enough to attend her Catechism class. She forgets to tell me this, so I'm lolling in our green bath listening to Birthday Requests on Radio Ceylon when Mignon tok-toks into our room, throwing me a foul look.

'Only trying to clean myself up… since I'm in-digi-nut…' I murmur under cover of Connie Francis crooning 'Where the Boys Are!' on the tinny wireless. When Mignon turns on her stiletto, I mime a hideous face.

'Pox-marked witch with baggy armpits! As if I care, to not be allowed into upside-down-Australia!'

Some minutes later the car doors slam on the drive. Wheels pulling away assure me that I've been left on my own!Connie   shimmies on while I sink my head under the water.

A smiling face, a warm embrace…
Two arms to hold me tender-leeeeeyy!
Wheeeere the boy's aaah…

Dinner at Casa Bianca is grown up and glittery. The chandelier glows through mauve-pink trumpet flowers. The silent battery of servants—who never look you in the eye—move swiftly, scared of being hit from behind. I have yet to hear them utter a sound in the three weeks we've been stuck with this virago who is using my mother to get something out of Quintus?

When I ask why Casa Bianca staff do not talk—even to each other—Selma says,

'Why do you think, child? She had their tongues removed when they came from their village.'

I thought she was joking because of the way she said it. Now I'm not so sure. The only one who is allowed to keep his tongue is the head boy. He has to answer the telephone and relay messages from Quintus—Mignon's husband—who she has not spoken to in three years. Dinner is the only meal Quintus is wheeled downstairs for, though he hardly eats enough to feed a Myna bird. Perched at the head of the table he enjoys recollecting life before his stroke.

I like to think of life *before* Casa Bianca. Mignon keeps her malachite eyes focussed in the other direction so as not to glimpse him.

If Quintus chats to Selma too long, Mignon mutters through clenched teeth 'Stroke of luck, that's what!'

15

The boys—changed into starched sarongs and Nehru tunics— move the vase of Arum lilies off the Indian Elm dining table to make space for decorative Venetian oil and vinegar bottles. They do this every night with solemnity, like altar boys arranging the communion chalice for Padre. If they scratch these rare items it won't be just their tongues they lose. I watch them light the candles in silver holders before I inspect my only friends here, the ants, returning to their anthill on the other side of the low parapet wall. Their city is in this Jam-Fruit tree. These massive insects with a double bump on their head are worse than the deadly Coddiya ants. Other people's servants tell stories of how in remote villages, when someone is punished for serious misdeeds they get tied to the ant tree. The victim dies when their tongue swells and chokes them. I keep a safe distance from the anthill, but I'm fascinated by the insect labourers.

A gentle putt-putt of a motor. Leaping up on the parapet, I see a man on a scooter already halfway down the drive. As he gets close, I notice a clerical collar. He sees me and waves before pulling up under the portico, as if he owns the place. The priest disentangles his cassock from his bicycle clips and comes toward me briskly, holding out his hand.

'Hello, I'm Father Ignatius. Will you tell your mother I'm here?'

He thinks I am Mignon's daughter.

'They aren't back yet. Would you like to go to the library?'

(I catch myself from saying lie-berry in time)

The silent boys don't show up so I must lead the guest upstairs. A faint whiff of clove cologne drifts over. He must be a regular visitor or used to such grand places. He asks if I play tennis, as he takes the stairs two at a time.

'There's a decent court here, you know. Hardly gets used…' I think I hear him sigh.

'I wish I had someone to play with. I don't know any children here and I haven't a clue how to—hold a bat…'

'A racket.'

Blood gushes to my cheeks.

'Racket, I mean-' I feel idiotic. 'I'm not, I'm not Mignon's daughter, I'm…'

'I think I know who you are!' The Father's teeth are flakes of blue-white salt.

We reach the landing. He fixes me with a curious smile. I'm spitting mad I said bat instead of racket. The priest taps and opens the library door. I watch Quintus's expression switch from that of a frail old man.

'What brings you, old cock?' Quintus holds out his good arm like a child wanting a hug.

The Father advances and does just that. He embraces him tight. For a whole minute Quintus says nothing but wheezes and taps his one hand on the priest's back. His eyes are glistening when his voice lets him croak

'Iggy! So, you scraped past the drawbridge? Darn good to see you, Boyo-'

The door shuts. I stand rooted, wondering where I've heard that name? Iggy…

I perch my bum on the polished brass handrail from habit, letting myself slide down. Iggy? Yes, Mignon was going on about Iggy-this and Iggy-that but I'd imagined the name belonged to a fortune teller crone. Not a name of a young priest? As I skip down the carpeted steps, I hear the crunch on gravel announce Princess Rhino returning with Selma.

Oops! Is this a Father from another church to the one I've been made to wait at, these past weeks? Have I taken her secret priest and delivered him to her enemy? That, added to missing my penance of waiting at the monastery will be reason to tie me to the ant tree. As soon as car doors slam, Mignon is yelling at her silent boys. Clearly still cross with my mother for making them late.

She struts past me. I have guilt on my face.

'And…. what have you been up to?' Mignon's eyes narrow to slits. I paste myself to the wall to give her room.

'We missed the ruddy appointment. Even priests won't wait forever. Have you… been taking my perfume, little wretch?'

'No?'

'Then why are you looking sheepish?'

I melt further into the wall 'Um, Fa-Father Ignatius has come…'

'Huh? He's *here!*' The cold jade chips light up sixty watts.

I take a breath, but it's gone before I finish the sentence. 'While he was waiting… he went to the li-berry.' This time I say it how she expects. Give her something to carp at.

'*Library!* How will she get you past the Keep Australia White test with you still speaking like a savage?'

Mignon's lips untwist as she calls to my mother over her shoulder and swings up the stairs. She replaces her doorstop earrings, beaming so wide her mask will surely crack to reveal those hollow crevices filled with pancake makeup. Quintus is laughing softly on the other side of the door when she reaches the landing. She can't invade his territory. Mignon turns, her forefinger pointing its red dagger upwards like a weather vane. As her dumb waiters carry dishes from the kitchen to the electric trolley, she calls an order in stilted Sinhala asking them to prepare an extra place.

My spine tingles! I shoot upstairs to steal Mignon's scent and to find my new ankle socks.

Quintus sits at the head of the table. His crumpled body has a new energy. Selma is between Quintus and Father. I am placed opposite our guest of honour, the Jesuit with a haircut like Fabian—the big girl's pin-up at school. I can feast on his lively brown face, so animated even when he's talking seriously.

Mignon's glacial stare is defrosting. She can't ignore Quintus tonight! I giggle inside. Selma with her Geisha hair-do is flirting, laughing over any jokes going, mostly her own. I could swear they had used some yellowish face powder, a bad match for my mother's skin. Mignon has not learnt when to laugh, or how.

Father Ignatius has a natural knack of weaving me into their conversation, keeping me on my toes. When he breaks off to explain a point, he doesn't talk down at you. If only other adults did that. My cheeks are glued into a grin, reminding me of my very first time on a Merry-Go-Round.

When Quintus dozes in his chair, we move to the drawing room with a polished floor like dark chocolate. Iggy drops onto the rug to help me with the final pieces of the jigsaw. The servant wheeling Quintus into the room carefully places a cushion on the side of his neck.

'Phew—thanks Father! Its trickier than the one I got for my last birthday.'

'Which month is yours?'

'August.'

'First week?'

'How d'you guess?'

'Me too. I'm not just a priest you know. I'm a mind reader!'

Mignon is on the far side of the room, pouring coffee. In a flash she is at Iggy's elbow, teeth glinting like he's an after-dinner mint.

'Aaah… Father must come to your party!' she purrs, licking those non-existent lips. 'You'll come to the child's birthday, surely?'

'Here? What - a kid's party?' His disbelieving frown mocks her. He must know how she loves children!

'Where else? Ten years. Must celebrate that!' Mignon turns to wink at my mother to convey her grand new idea. Selma is stunned, alarmed and suspicious.

'Young lady,' Father offers a hand to help me off the floor, 'I'm honoured to be invited… however, let it be known…' he glares at Mignon '…I am not in the habit of attending parties for ten-year olds'

Mignon, head bowed, backs to the sideboard. Father Ignatius begins to leave, despite his hostess trying to tempt him to a stemmed glass of something else.

'If I have one more glass, ladies, my scooter will have to ride me home!' Iggy smooths his cassock and tenderly drops an air-kiss over the head of Quintus, now snoring like a baby.

It is only then that I see them!

The entire silent squadron are lined up behind each other in the highly polished hallway. At the end of the queue are two garden boys—usually not allowed indoors under any circumstances. What makes them brave it in front of the Jesuit? They are not Christian, yet they press their hands together in prayer?

I dare not look at Mignon. I'm worried she will whip off her stiletto and clobber them for insolence.

Koki-Appa, our ancient cook, wears a curved tortoise-shell comb like a back-to-front tiara. This is worn in remote villages by only senior men; I have seen these ornate head combs in the illustrations of history books. The Koki, lame and three times the age of the priest, struggles to prostrate himself to the Jesuit. One by one, the boys all follow suit.

Iggy is clearly accustomed to people swooning, kissing his feet. He knows their names and places his hands on each of the boys head as they rise, tracing a cross on their forehead:

'Loku-Banda.
Sunil, hari hari.
Ah, Muthu-Malli?
Siri.
Athul. Dhang hondai the?
Mathew, Umma commada?
Janaka? Enne ko-
Kumar… ah! Raheem. God-bless!'

Their reverence is unmistakable as they receive his blessing in such fast Latin (it sounds like Tamil to me).

Father Ignatius exits like an actor leaving his stage after curtain call. He does not glance at Mignon. His scooter putt-putts into the starry night, leaving his devotees of Buddhist, Muslim and Hindu faiths anointed. The boys lock their hands in tribute until the scooter growl gets devoured by the deafening hymn of the crickets.

My heartbeat explodes in my chest, drumming *I love you! I love you!*

A RUBY THE SIZE OF THE RITZ

I wouldn't say a thing to Carla about what a jerk our host is. Holidays at his hill villa had been fun. We hadn't met Carla then. I lapped up whatever our generous friend laid on when Mum brought me here from boarding school. Vickrama's villa was a 2-hour drive along the hairpin bends through tea estate roads, whereas getting to Colombo entailed two bus rides, a long train journey and a taxi to whoever was daft enough to put up with an impoverished seamstress and her brat.

      Uncle Vickrama was an amiable host with a houseful of servants. Twenty-eight, he looked thirty-eight and dressed forty-eight. He had a fridge stacked with Kit Kats. I had little idea they were bait. Yes, everything changed on the holiday Carla tagged along because she let the cat out of the bag.

Sitting next to me at breakfast, she asked in a pass-the-salt way if I were looking forward to my engagement? Through the French windows our host and Mum discussed the new shrubs with the gardener, having been awake long before us. *Engagement?*

'Who? Me? I'm …twelve!' I gasped.

I had always called our host 'Uncle' Vickrama, though he was no Uncle of mine. Carla's question was insane. I searched her face for a clue this might be one of her sadder jokes, but Carla wore the you-can-confide-in-me look so craftily.

'What are you talking about?'

'Well yes… you are the chosen one, it seems,' she said a mite too fast. In that second, I knew that not only was this no joke, but Carla was a titch envious. Carla, the sophisticated divorcee, my mother billed her to our friends, as if it entailed some glamour from another world. Carla, with the luxury apartment at the Galle Face Court overlooking the Indian Ocean. Vivacious Carla, whose snazzy cocktail frocks were stamped with London labels and who visited the Salon at the Intercontinental to keep her hair immaculate. Could a grown woman be envious of a 12-year-old who hadn't grown armpit hair and was last in the class to warrant a teenage bra?

I pushed the *kiributh* to the corner of my plate along with the cardamom pods. The *lunu-miris* sambal was too salty. I recalled a peculiar face Carla had pulled when Mum first mentioned Vickrama. That he was an old-fashioned gent. An eldest son in line to inherit a small Portuguese mansion with rubber estates outside Colombo, and a house in the hills. How Carla had yawned extravagantly and then gone quiet. Next thing I knew, she was eager to accompany us for half-term break.

'I realise you can't tell any school chums about this—given Vicky's position. Mum must have warned you not to talk to just anybody… but you know, I'm like family. It's why your mother trusts me enough to invite me…'

I reached for the rough pottery bowl of buffalo curd but it was practically empty. I stared through Carla as she burbled on.

'I want you to know you can chat to me about…' she took a lunge at her coffee and reached for my hand on the table as if we were buddies, '..anything at all.'

I pasted a grateful smile. I wasn't sure if I could trust this glamour-puss pal of Mum, who'd provided her with lucrative commissions to run up copies of Bond Street frocks in two sizes larger. There was nobody I could talk to about her loony idea till I had the chance to speak to Sis. She was working in the Middle-East providing the money to pay for my school at the mission-run boarding. Sis would know if this was Carla's imagination but she only called us once a month.

My cousin married a man of her choice at twenty-one. I was aware of families arranging marriages to match the Caste system of Tamils and Sinhala. Marina, my Parsee friend and sure-fire netball star, stopped school in the middle of term when her periods began at eleven and a half. The next time we glimpsed her was in a shoe shop with an aunt. Marina was enveloped in a dowdy mustard Salwar kameez. She answered meekly that she had to be married to a business-friend of her father's. Although Marina lived two blocks from the Methodist church school attended by Buddhists, Hindus, Christians and Muslim girls studying in the English medium, her family did not allow her to return.

Marina, with her large liquid eyes, vanished from the earth before collecting her end of term report.

Mum told me nothing about what she was arranging behind the scenes with Vikrama. I was dimly aware she wished she'd been young enough to pair herself with this solid citizen, as she called him.

For as long as I can remember, my mother's distant dream was to save every cent to get us to England. The new government had announced a Sinhala Only programme to ban English from schools. Many with English mother-tongue were panicking to reach countries where their children could continue schooling without restriction. It was pushing mum towards the land of plenty, where she believed the pavements were studded with TV sets.

I didn't see how that dream could fit the ridiculous idea about Uncle Vickrama. I recalled he once told her earnestly he would only consider a wife who had been brought up with English. So, for a single woman with no security—marrying me off to Uncle Vicky might be her nifty Pension Plan? My resentment towards my mother found its way out in obstreperous behaviour. I overheard a telephone conversation about an Engagement when I turned fourteen and realised, with alarm, that they did mean business.

I ran away from school.

I had to return the same day, because now Carla was not to be trusted, I didn't even have a place to run to.

Mum was livid that I refused to be compliant and dragged me off to our parish priest. He suggested Confirmation may rein in my 'difficult' behaviour. She wasn't letting Reverend McIntyre in on her negotiations with Uncle Vickrama! A lacy Confirmation frock mum was sewing kept reminding me of a wedding dress. I had not imagined my life could be stitched up in this way.

The Fab Four were pumping out *Please, Please me!* on the Radio. I yearned to ice-skate, to learn The Twist, to see The Beatles live! I dreamed of a boyfriend who looked like Adam Faith.

Finally, Mum begged and borrowed sufficient for the very cheapest passage. On the ship which conveyed us to Southampton, I chummed up with a bunch of cheeky, Australian youngsters from whom I picked up swear words. They smoked stolen ciggies on the corner of the Quoits deck and never missed a session of the folk foursome from Melbourne who sang:

There's a new world somewhere,
they call the promised land

27

and I'll be there someday if you will hold my hand…

We couldn't guess that within a year these four-The Seekers - would become the first Ozzy group to top the UK charts. When the disco music took over, their dishy guitarist Keith Potger asked me to dance. He towered above me as I showed off what I had picked up of The Twist. The Ozzy teenagers blinked enviously since he didn't dance with them. I wanted to be part of this new world, including swear words. While the band took a break, the girls crammed into the nearest toilet to fawn over the singer, Judith, while she checked her teeth for lipstick smudges.

After the first few brushes in the Ladies, I got brave enough to chat while she teased her beehive hair. She said she was nearing her twenty-first birthday; it was her first trip outside Australia and she'd been working as a secretary before she found she had a voice.

Uncle Vickrama showed up in London three months ahead of my fourteenth birthday. I was half a head taller. He hadn't grown. It was 1962. I felt strangely at ease in the bustle of Swinging London.

Against the street scene of lanky, long-haired youths in bell bottoms and poser Twiggy-types strutting *Couregges* boots, Vicky, wearing an old-style suit with narrow lapels, was an elephant at a disco. I was embarrassed to be seen with such a 'square'.

Mum gave orders to accompany Uncle Vicky round London ending with a walk in St James's Park. We sat at opposite ends of a bench, Vickrama grinning expectantly.

'So, how you are liking U-kay, then? Are the boys very forward? My word, I hear they try French kissing even at bus stops…'

I stifled a groan. Uncle Vicky fumbled in his carrier bags for a plump, velvet jeweller's box. He switched a serious face on, mouthing words I could not catch. Didn't want to hear. Inside the box was a ring with a gem the size of my thumbnail. It glared at me. My ears were filled with a high-pitched whine. This was... an *engagement* ring? Uncle Vickrama seemed to be an expert on precious stones: this gem was bought on his parent's Ruby anniversary in Rangoon. Although Ceylon Sapphires, Aquamarines, Rubies and Emeralds were prized the world over, he said, gem connoisseurs considered a Pigeon's Blood ruby from Burma renowned for its unique colour. He may as well have ranted about the Cricket Score.

Uncle Vickrama went solemn as he pressed it onto my finger and asked that I scrap the 'Uncle' and call him Vicky. After all, we were going to be man and wife in one year, nine months. He grinned slyly, waiting for it to sink in.

My mind went blank. I couldn't speak. Two ladies trotting past in matching silver-grey twinsets with name tags and Dr Scholl sandals saw the ring and their mouths hung open.

The ducklings knew how I felt and quacked their condolences.

'Cute, aren't they?' he tried to catch my eye.

The next spot on the itinerary arranged by mum was Harrods. Vicky had been told it was *the* place the Queen bought her groceries, where Lords and Ladies went for Tea. Mum heard this from one of the sisters-in-law who lodged with us at Seven Sisters Road where we crammed into a front parlour-turned-bedroom. I paced several steps ahead of Vickrama, hoping to lose him on the escalator between floors. I let myself wander into the plush Edwardian Ladies on the first floor with antique fittings from another era. Staring at my reflection in the soft lighting, I thought of my lovely Marina, probably already married to her father's business associate? I was uneasy washing my hands with a ring that size.

When I finally joined him on the fourth floor, Vickrama looked pleased with himself. He made some joke: he thought I had been kidnapped by another handsome man. He added that he had commissioned an artist—through Harrods Portrait department—to paint my portrait! The manager of the department came to shake hands (I thought he did a double-take for the resemblance between 'father' and 'daughter') while explaining, that it usually took around four sittings with the portrait Artist in the studio. He showed us samples of completed works awaiting collection in gaudy gilt frames. One that caught my eye was of an olive-skinned girl like me, in a Yashmak, with eyes that were shiny and scared, like Marina. She was urging me to stand up for myself. To get the hell out of there!

Somewhere between the Perfume Hall and the Edwardian Ladies Room secreted on the first floor, the Burmese Pigeon Blood ruby floated off my finger.

Amidst the sweat and tears that weekend, Mum came close to pulling her hair out by the roots. How would she account to her Solid Citizen that I had lost his highly prized Pigeon Blood ruby? The shock of it stunned her into thinking what she was pushing me into. Yet it was too good a chance to let go of someone she regarded as an enviable catch. I didn't give a hoot about his ring, but it pained me to watch my mother edging towards a nervous breakdown. What was it that she wasn't telling me? Was she in debt to our crook uncle whose rooms we rented? The family had warned her how he snatched at every innocent new arrival's savings for his illicit schemes. An 'Asian Peter Rackman' they called him. Is this why she was having to off-load me on this middle-aged, grey-suited suitor?

One of the lodger girls asked, 'Now has anyone even phoned the shop to see if they found the ring?'

We stared at the youngest sister-in-law in astonishment.

'This is England after all! People who find things like purses actually give it to the Lost and Found department, you don't know anything, do you? Even on London Transport, Yers!'

With trembling hands Mum telephoned the Lost Property Office at Baker Street. No luck. Then she dialled Harrods.

Indeed, a matron from the shires had handed in a ring with a dark red stone she found on the wash basin of the Edwardian Powder Room.

Vickrama and Mum managed small talk over cups of orangey brown liquid at The Ceylon Tea Centre near Leicester Square. They agreed that tea tasted better brewed in a pot.

'Ah, but English people… what can they know about making tea?' he said lamely.

Maybe he didn't realise it was a very young Brit, James Taylor who, disagreeing with his boss on a coffee plantation, gave Tea its first attempt on a scrap of land in Loolecondra. We'd been taught about this innovative 16-year-old, single-handedly responsible for creating a whole new industry, when the coffee blight wrecked thousands of acres on the island. There was such a chasm between the man my mother wanted to marry me off to, and the person I was after five months in London.

Mum, a paler version of her former self, tried not to show her eagerness to relinquish the 4.02 carat jewel back to its owner. She offered the excuse she had rehearsed:

'I've come to realise that your young lady is not quite mature enough, so should we…. postpone the engagement say, for another… year, Vicky, dear?'

My intended husband sucked in his cheeks, making a sound like a tyre deflating; he threw me a hapless grin. He could hardly argue. Mum and I kept to our pact: not to let on about the loss of the gem or our hectic search all weekend. There was an awkward silence while Vickrama folded his ruby back into its satin-lined casket. He edged closer, made that flat tyre noise again and assured me he was coming to visit next year to *see about things*. His head did a jolly dance, nodding sideways as he clumsily grabbed at my hand: he promised me to set a date for our wedding then!

I was grateful he agreed to a postponement until my fifteenth birthday so I tried not to yank my hand away.

Vickrama asked if I'd care to finish the last curry puff?

I took miniscule bites of a pastry I had no desire to eat.

Like many of the Windrush generation's progeny, I had to enter Britain on my mother's passport. I did not feel entitled to a voice, never mind a passport of my own. Helplines had not entered our vocabulary. I didn't know where to ask advice. I did not even know that I was entitled to it. Even worse, I had no clue that what my mother was forcing me to do was illegal!

I pushed aside the greasy curry puff, and I asked for a toasted crumpet please? Mum and Vicky were happy to chomp on imitation curry puffs and samosas which tasted like sawdust compared to the ones we'd left behind. I had learnt there was no beating a hot, buttery, crumpet with Marmite. When it arrived, I used both pats of butter on it. Vickrama and my mother looked disdainfully on while I watched the Irish butter melt into the holes.

I knew that by handing back Vickrama's heirloom I had bought 365 days of my life back. What would become of me after that?

How long before I learn to melt into the holes and not be seen?

UPSTAIRS FOR INSANITY

Insanity—a perfectly rational adjustment to an insane world ~ R. D. Laing.

Until I turned up at the Harley Street clinic, I had not heard of R. D. Laing.

Why would I? I was on a mission: to extract my confiscated passport and return to Rome.

The old-fashioned brass elevator rattled to the fourth floor, giving me a whooshy feeling in my stomach. It could have been hunger? Or anxiety. What should I say to him? Why would he want to help? Patrizia, who arranged the meeting, told me this doctor was a famous consultant. His waiting list for clients was booked six months ahead. Despite the fact he was about to leave on a lecture tour of America in a week or two, she had pleaded for him to squeeze me in. Patrizia said proudly that she did her thesis on R. D. Laing!

A famous psychoanalyst has agreed to see me without charging a fee. So here I was on a dull, drizzly day, being shown to see Mr Ronnie Laing.

Sounds a good name for a jazz pianist.

The door of the cage lift that surfaced on the fourth floor was opened by another receptionist in an identical white uniform—like nurses from a Hollywood musical. Any moment they would join hands, do a backflip into an aquamarine pool and tra-la *By a waterfall we're calling you hu – hu - huuuu*!

Both ladies had the same spidery eyelashes; like dolls forced to stay awake. But no melodies arose from her puckered lips. She became terse as I looked about.

'This stops here, Miss Adriana. Mr Laing's rooms are on the fifth floor…'   My fantasy of a Busby Berkley dancer hesitatingly led me up further stairs with a different vintage of stair carpet: grey, worn, in need of a vacuum cleaner. The air was mustier. I followed Spider Lashes in her designer clogs I'd seen in an airport shop for £200.

The lighting here was of lower wattage. In the hospital I had escaped from —the same one The Pope was in eight months back—they assigned me my own round-the-clock security guard to stand on the balcony. To make sure I did not jump. When the TV Roma crew charged in, the guard became flabbergasted. He was outside on the tiny balcony. They were running wild inside. He had not been briefed what to do about them. He'd been put there to guard *me*.

Spider Lashes murmured something like 'nearly there'. I got the feeling we had proceeded past the threshold of the 44-guineas a go. These stairs were creakier, the cobwebs grew to art installations. Alarm may have shown on my face because she lurched at a wide wooden door, rapped on it.

The stink of a Barons Court bedsit and burnt toast. Without waiting for an answer, Spider Lashes opened the door, ushered me in, then shuts it. I hear her footsteps scuttle away.

Back to civilization where she could practise her tap dance with the rest of the fake-nurses. It takes time for my eyes to adjust to the dim lighting. I was in a cavernous attic room—easily a side wing of Gormenghast.

I couldn't make out a figure, but I heard a tenor voice from behind a cloud of pipe smoke.   'I'm over here… by the window…'

Light headed, I needed to sit. Just that short walk from Warren Street tube has been too much for my still untreated, dislocated hip. My injured shoulder and neck are making my body hurt like an old woman's. I had left Rome in panic and desperation. In a wheelchair, now lost. Both wheelchair and myself.

'Find yourself somewhere to perch,' a man in a tweed jacket said, sensing my trepidation. He had wild dark eyebrows, a high forehead like an opera singer. I had been expecting someone ancient.

I struggled to reach him and hand over the precious envelope, then lunged into the only chair without stacks of magazines or newspapers. I managed to spit my name out.

'Ah yes… Patrizia's friend? Yes…' He was peering through smudgy spectacles at the contents of my therapist's letter.

I looked round counting eight half-empty coffee mugs of various age. The shambles were reassuring, I supposed; like the shambles of my life.

'And how long had you been consulting… with Patrizia when you had this… accident?' he said at last, like a headmaster who feels sorry I'd not passed the cxam. In those few words he conveyed a kindness that warmed me to him.

Was this some kind of actor pretending to be a world-famous shrink? His natural impishness made me relax and feel at ease with this stranger.

'Ah? No, we only met when she turned up… in the hospital…'

'Is that so?' he spoke in a sort of Glaswegian lilt. Would I have known what that sounds like—never been north of Turnpike Lane?

A clock chimed three, then a minute later two more clocks made their own admission for three, forcing me to raise my voice.

'She appeared at my bedside… she'd been sent by…ummm-'

'Someone you knew?' He had his pen poised on a sheet of headed notepaper.

'Well… she came like a dream... Just to have someone who could speak English in a hospital full of Italians was …'

'Mmmn, Yes, yes.' His eyes held genuine curiosity. He wanted to know what I was talking about. Even if I didn't know.

'I hadn't actually met Patrizia. Er… no, I had met a dear, old couple—not Italians— sort of - a pair of nice grandparents I wish I'd had… some months before all this. And lost track of them. They read about my accident in the papers, remembered me and then asked Patrizia if there was something she might do to help?' I was surprised I could string that many words and feel puffed out in relief.

I thought he was waiting for me, but I'd forgotten what came next.

'I'm not sure why you wanted to leave there?' he asked, alert and curious.

'I wanted to leave this planet! They said they'd have to throw me in prison, if not that I was under age….'

R.D. Laing held onto his jaw as if it needed propping up. 'Oh? Of course, it's a Catholic country, I see what you mean…'

'I was lucky that t…'

'Did they warn you they would regard it as a crime?'

'It is. Suicide is a crime there! I hadn't a clue about that. Wouldn't have stopped me'

'Umm, I see.'

'The newspapers made up so many stories, the Italians were being simpatico…'

'So how did police get involved?'

'Particularly the police! They were trying to help me get out without being arrested. I didn't understand what anyone was saying—my colloquial Roman is enough to say a few words on the film set. I didn't understand civil servant Italian. Anyway, this was two days after the fall…'

'Six floors.' He shook his head, disbelieving that the wreck from that disaster was sitting neatly before him in a black knit dress.

'Seven floors.' I corrected. 'Top floor of the Hilton. I couldn't understand any Italian at this point… I was disappointed to *be* alive…'

Silence.

R. D. Laing's pipe had gone out. There was some shuffling. A match was struck. His ineptitude lighting it almost made me giggle; was he practising with a prop for his scene in a play that evening? Somehow, I didn't think smoking a pipe matches this man? I wondered what sort of test he would set me—to see whether I was mad.

When he spoke it was like a song. It felt as if a warming balm was going through my chest. I inhaled it.

'Did they give you an interpreter? Was there anyone from your Embassy?'

'Embassy? I didn't think I could ask… I could barely remember my name—this was before Patrizia arrived. I had nobody to talk on my behalf... I don't know if they stopped my friends coming in?'

'I see. How very inhospitable… to be in a…' he stopped himself saying 'hospital' just as we both heard it coming.

'My passport is not British, it's from the Romanian Embassy. They've confiscated it, the bu'- I stopped myself in time.

'Ah?' This seemed to be noteworthy.

'When the ambulance took me I was herded into the government hospital. Crowded and chaotic. Some friends—I found out later—took a hat round to pay for me to move to the private block. I don't even know which friends, to thank them…'

The famous Mr Laing took a sheet of paper and wrote, but continued to listen intently as I warbled on. It was probably the first time in my life someone was genuinely interested in hearing me. What a great trick, if this were an actor, pretending to be the psychoanalyst?

'Headlines in La Stampa claimed "*Un miracolo!*" Even the doctors did not comprehend how three attempts and 58 barbiturates somehow left me alive. I was "caught by an angel" an ambulance man who found me naked on the grass, was quoted as saying. *Corriere dela Serra* made out that a thwarted love affair with "un Lordo Inglesi" was the cause of it.

'-oh? where did they-'

'Then the Communist daily *L'Unita* - wrote more nonsense after they stormed into my flat and spotted a Che Guevara poster on my kitchen wall…'

'Did they really? You have been very fortunate…' He was pressing his mouth to stop a small laugh, I thought.

Well, it certainly seemed funny. Even to the victim, the perpetrator, the girl who had defied a fall of 70 feet onto the hard ground.

'I was fodder for any paper or magazine. There was no shortage of snappers to sell the newspapers photos of me. On the set doing PR photos, off the set. So virtually every magazine in Italy had me on its cover by the second week.'

'Why, er- yes, did you choose that particular hotel? It's quite a way outside the city, isn't it?' He must have been there to know that.

'Sure. It's well outside. I hardly had the taxi fare to get there that day. I chose the Rome Hilton because it *was* so remote. I was there for an audition once with my agent; she and I got lost from the Ladies toilets and she'd said, *Madonna mia, this-a place! Upstairs the bedrooms even worse, hah! You can die here an nobody come an' find you for a-one week-a? Porca miseria!*

'I remembered that. Seemed ideal for my purpose. I'd too easily have been discovered in my Trastevere flat, you see. Too many bods passing through wanting a random glimpse of my famous neighbour who lived opposite in Via dei Genovesi - Maria Callas, frequently snapped by Il Paparazzi on the arm of her Playboy Onassis.'

I was now drained after so much talking. I could have easily snuggled into a corner for a nap. I hope I didn't doze? My head clears as I hear his melodious voice again. I think he's saying, '…lucky to be alive?'

41

'Not really, I wanted to be gone! When they discovered I was still under twenty-one, the policeman at my bedside who were fatherly types, they suggested I leave Italy—for a month or two. They told my mother - who couldn't understand a word they were saying – that they were prepared to close the case….if we somehow bugger off -'

'Yes?' his eyes were out on stalks. I was sure he thought I was making it up.

'And need not chuck me behind bars…so that's when we left -mum and I - left in a hurry'

I was worrying how this must sound to this kind, head-masterly Mr Laing. A script from a cheap film - my bread and butter until I started getting hired by Cinecitta.

He nodded several times, seemingly moved at my plight.

'Humane police? Yers….That is touching'

'I could hardly believe them! It was incredible that they thought of a way out for me? Then some busybody got my mother worried that if I went back to the movie biz, I might try - er, this again…'

He passed the envelope to me with a concerned look.

'Well, good luck with it,' he said brightly, giving me permission to leave his study.

I was sure I'd forgotten to thank him. I felt overwhelmed that there was no more to it. No test of my madness? If I told him anymore, he might have wanted to take me home and feed me macaroni cheese and give me a woolly pair of socks to put on my freezing feet. I edged away trying not to knock any of the stale coffee mugs over.

I did not dare open this precious document until I reached the flat where I was sofa-surfing in Sloane Gardens. A place I had been offered by a kind girl I'd never met before.

In his own handwriting R. D. Laing confirmed that he had today examined Miss Adriana Savante and was suitably assured that she is of sound mind.

Armed with this priceless document, I had to continue my battle against the Embassy who had confiscated the passport my mother stole out of my bag after arriving in London. I had nowhere but that fragmented life in Rome, which pushed me to take the leap. Until I returned there and found work, I couldn't even afford the fee of the British passport I had been told I might apply for.

The place where I had thrown myself off the seventh floor was the only home I knew.

BEAUTIFUL, GOOD, AND ALL WHAT FOR?

Many time I am seeing Santa Tierra.

Our aunties and my sister can't help say Dilukshi—then they catch themself like a swear word slipping out. The holy name divined for her at Carmelite Convent on that high-up hill where ordinary person can't go essept one time a year, is Santa Tierra.

In our village the families of girls she at school with, getting big shock when she becoming Bride of Christ two weeks before her seventeen celebration. The money she and she's young man saving for marriage chest she's family giving to Carmelite Sisters. That happen after Santa Tierra struck dumb and climb the pilgrims thorn path to the Carmelites. *Aparade, aney!*

Hot and rocky up that hill, climbing for fifty minutes!

Red parched land is torching by devil he-self, old men say. No shade to protect pilgrims walking up. Inside the walls of convent, oranges with proper orange skin— same like imported fruit—are growing!

How? Convent have magic earth because this fruit is sweet like pani, goma-cart man is telling. Carmelite Sisters planting only Engal-ish vegetable; cabbage, beetroot, pot-ato, carrot, leek and herb. In some month after rainy season, so much extra growing that they sending in bullock cart by that man taking them goma from his buffalo to grow this nice fat vegetable. If our Santa Tierra loose rest of her life doing penance, her mother will satisfy she feed fresh food for God's sake! This what my Ammi saying every night after she kneeling to make special prayer for Santa.

Why Ammi want pray for good people like her? Santa Tierra have no time to do sins, *aney!* When Angel talkings beginning, that time Santa Tierra's eyes getting red. She cannot get up from bed after sleeping—legs have no life, it seems. Saying the light is too bright! I am thinking she mean the light round those Angels? I still a small girl when she taken to Carmelite Sisters, but I feel a stone in my heart—like a death. Even though I not knowing any person to die.

In evening time when cool enough to go loafing, my sister taking gunny-sack to collect dry goma pats we finding by road. This Ammi is happy for; to burn in fire, to put on her manioc plants. For many, many months every evening they make me walk with them past that hill to see Santa Tierra's lonely place where she now invisible from us. Sister and Ammi just stand looking as if suddenly window will open and she fly out!

Me thinking about the big drought when buffalo all stop giving milk and everybody cattle dying, how our Santa Tierra save them! Yes, for true. She having voice so high like Shama bird that sing from the thorn-apple tree. I know some sounds human peoples not hearing. That is how her voice is. When she singing sweetly to the baby buffalo, they doing a dance and running to their mother: they love her voice every morning. When they hear it, milk is starting from mothers like rain coming after the dry season.

This first time for peoples thinking something bad happening ...

Then she taken to become Bride of Christ. So much sad occasion you cannot believe, ah? That is last time the family can see her until she become old and die. After this, poor people's living in cadjan huts by the river, coming all the way to Puwakapitiya to say their stories outside church: stories we not allow to listen about the men from don't-know-where holding those lightening sticks, this big! And then somebody ask; why all the pilgrim walking up to convent never returning? What happen there? Who is keeping hold of those poor pilgrim?

I decide already I not growing up too much good girl, too much clever; otherwise, see what happen, no? I see same thing as our Santa Tierra, only I too frighten to say - no never in my life!

'I don't know what for, divine child have her life chopping off at seventeen-year,' Ammi say.

'Ammi, she not locked away!' My sister, two years senior to Santa Tierra have her own idea 'Her life just begin no? She destined. Like great Opera singer she training to -'

'Training? What kind training, what is this?' Ammi ready to give one big slap.

How my sister speaking like she is such expert knowing everything? After that day when man in safari-suit come to factory in big car and putting brown envelope with American dollars in her hand, she now talking like a crazy *pissu*!

When I stay outside waiting for her to finish work, I have seen man with feet that not touching ground! Not even like a human I thinking then, but I no tell nothing: me am sensible girl. In that kapura factory, where they stinking their clothes, hair, skin, making camphor-ball from dawn till night time, coming back coughing-coughing, nobody allow to talk like my sister.

So, what for I must to tell what I seen?

THE CURD MAKER

They say that no one makes curd like I do. Mum and I used to make it for *seva*. People say our Mum made divinely creamy curd because she had a big heart.

When she first brought us to India, we stayed in Goa in an old Portuguese villa with a sandpit under a Banyan tree. Brat and I turned the Banyan tree into our cafe. We offered travellers returning from the beach, jellies and cakes carved from wet sand; payment was sea shells. When I got bored of childish stuff, I learned to make real curd from buffalo milk.

My brother Krishna and I used to play happily before this journey to the Ganges. When Mum announced her idea to our Godparents before leaving Wiltshire, I was surprised when she said we were going to drown Brat in the river. I was sad he would sink to the bottom after we threw flower petals and waved him goodbye.

But soon it evolved into a daydream. One I enjoyed dwelling on whenever he annoyed me. I was disappointed when he only had a dunk in the Ganges for his seventh birthday with noisy loudspeakers chanting from all directions.

By the time we reached this crowded Ashram with its tower blocks wedged between a fast-rushing river and the ferocious ocean, far too risky to swim in, I knew life would be easier without Brat to attract attention with his monkey tricks. His magic. Now that Mum has gone, he's a massive pain in the butt.

Neptune-Aunty, the lady who lives by the elevator on Neptune Block says, it's because he misses Mum. So, don't I count?

She asked us an odd question: 'Did your Mummy make a vow, child? Did she promise to hand you and Krishna to *Sadguru*?'

The old bat must think Mum has left Brat and me here forever.

This Ashram in Kerala has been home for almost a year. All Devotees of *Sadguru* have tasks: no one gets paid for doing *seva*. Mine is making curd for the International Cafe, so we're allowed a free breakfast on every day except Sunday. They have never had a child make the curd before. The pan containing 50 litres of milk needs two adults to lift it off the fire, that's why.

The overseas visitors who tire of the spicy, free ashram meals served out of aluminium buckets, get their fix of comfort food here. We used to go for chocolate pancakes with Mum, but now we have to make do with our freebie.

If I were older, they would not allow me to work while having a period. I'm tall for my age so I'm usually taken for a teenager. The Indian devotees don't tire of calling out, 'It's not your time of the month, suuuure? Not allowed kitchen duties, ah!'

This they repeat like a mantra every time I start my *seva*. I asked Neptune-Aunty (we don't know her real name) why they get so stressed: she shrugs.

'Unclean, no?' It's her answer to most things.

At weekends we have toast and Bovril with a mug of Milo when we join Neptune-Aunty on her tiny terrace to catch the sea breeze. Brat waters her plants as she lights camphor on dried coconut shells in a burner 'to purify us'. She can't be sure what germs we've picked up in the village where our school is. Incense alone won't get rid of the nits in my hair. Lucky that Neptune-Aunty is self-appointed monitor of my scalp. What will I do when she goes away June till August in the hot season? Neptune-Aunty is one of the few ashramas who owns her apartment for life. Mum had to pay the daily rate of 400 Rupees for room and food. She paid in advance so we attend the Hindi school where real Hindus will not send their children for fear foreigners such as our Danish and Dutch schoolmates might corrupt them!

Brat has got ace at foraging for things people leave behind. So we barter milkshake powder, cooking oil and tooth paste when foreign visitors turn up without supplies. Those who come for a month are the best bet; they often leave behind new clothes, shoes and once, a mango wood drum. Visitors from Bangalore and Bhubaneswar on festival days are the mingiest.

Though they politely call us Young Man and Young Lady when taking a photo, they can't believe we are alone and fend for ourselves.

Last week I helped a Bengali lady dressed in a grand sari over the footbridge to catch her boat. She asked how long I was staying?

'Until we find my mother! She went to do a course on... Trapeze... or maybe Taizé? We're not sure. We may still be here when you visit next.'

After her ferry-boat pulled away, I sank down on the muddy jetty and bawled my eyes out. That was the same boat Mum left on. I never cried then because we thought Mum was only staying away two weeks: she had paid Malti to babysit us in the meantime. I don't believe our Mum has left us; she loves us.

I know that for a fact.

We try using the washing lines on top of Lotus Block for best pickings. It is 16 floors high so Brown Eagles fly down to the rooftop at sunset. While I'm artfully scrounging shalwars or jeans between the flapping sheets I collide with Malti. In term-time she's one of the serious students of the Vet School that is funded by the Ashram. Malti organises our netball. She was looking for me to say a visiting *Swami* has requested to meet Brat and me!
That means I have to get my hair plaited by Neptune-Aunty - who is gagging to do the monthly de-louse. I can't bear climbing into the tight brown *shalwar kameez*—our school uniform. But that's all that fits me now apart from jeans.

If someone asks you to 'Tea' here it means no more than Marsala chai and a rusk. When we turn up at Eyebright Villa where the VIP's stay, I can't believe it! A table cloth, a tea pot, egg sandwiches made with mayonnaise, tinned fruit salad, two *laasis* from the Juice Bar are laid out on a concrete garden table! Just as well Brat had showered and gelled his hair. It was only Malti and us, though the feast was enough for five.

'How come, Krishna,' Malti says, stroking my newly dressed plaits, 'they don't make you shave your head like the others? You have a great shaped head, you know that?'

'Dunno. That's maybe because we're not Hindu,' he replies, scoffing his second sarnie.

'Not Hindu at all!' echoes a London voice behind us.

A white-robed *swami* sweeps in, touching my forehead and Krishna's in greeting. The air is filled with the same scent our Gran used. Channel *numero cinque* Mum called it.

I can't help staring at the white woman with shaved head and holy ash applied like misplaced makeup. Her deep blue eyes are ringed with purplish kohl.

'Heaven help us, Malti. So there's *two* of them?' She looks bemusedly from Krishna to me. Her eyebrows are like blond feathers stuck on.

The *Swami* plonks beside us in an easy-going manner.

Malti makes a signal indicating I should *Namaskaar* as we are drilled to do for holy people. I scramble up and yank Brat to his feet. *Swami* ruffles our hair.

'No need, children, since there's nobody but us...' She chats as though we've always known her. Peering to check who might be around, she laughs, showing she has done lots of laughing in her life.

'Tuck in before the flies descend... You certainly have your Mummy's eyes! Did you know, Parvati, Mummy used to bring you to my Yoga class in Wandsworth when you were a tiny baba? You were as good as gold, but as we got to the meditation at the end you'd grumble for your feed. Yes, let's finish the sarnies, Krish, we can't leave evidence of eggs being cracked in this holy place!'

My heart leaps. She knows our Mum, I mouth to brat. *She knows us!*

After tea Malti heads off for *Satsang*. Who needs wisdom when you have refills of pomegranate *laasi* (the priciest on the juice-bar list!)

We sit under the Ganeesha tree which smells of frangipani until the chanting from the naff new temple drowns the mosquito humming? *Swami-Ji* says she was sad to lose contact with Mum after she became ordained and left Wandsworth for Bihar, where her own mountain-top ashram is. She talks about many daughters and sons, one of whom—Kim—had been my only babysitter because Mum didn't trust anyone else with 'the dear tiny thing you were.'

It is comforting to talk to someone who knew Mum as her friend and me as a tiny thing. *Swami Lalleshwari* is not like the random strangers who tried to adopt us, such as the Scots couple who took us to Tamil Nadu for Holi celebrations. I couldn't stand how Brat mimicked his accent for weeks afterwards. I mentioned that Holi trip to him recently and d'you know, my brother couldn't remember this kind couple at all!

I used to think Brat had a piece missing. Now I envy his ability to blank people out so he won't be sad about them leaving. It's one way of coping. That is the word *Swami-Ji* used. She's alarmed *Sadguru* has let us be stranded without a parent these past months but says she is walking on eggshells. Whatever that means…

I think she doesn't want to make things awkward for Mum when she returns?

I can see why Mum liked *Swami-Ji* even before she became a *Swami*. Mum always had weird people for friends. Her eccentric ones told her not to trust our Papa. When my Papa asked her to marry him ten days before I was born, she was not thinking straight: she went ahead and married a middle-aged *Has-been,* up to his eyes in debt, when her friends warned her. Mum has repeated this conversation in such detail, on so many occasions I feel I was present with them, listening in. But I was tucked into a Perspex cot in the Prem Unit on the floor above her maternity ward in Old Hammersmith hospital; Yes, I surprised my parents by arriving seven weeks early! There was no way I could have witnessed this exchange. Yet I heard it!

I've thought of a name, mum says dreamily.
Papa is trying to find space for the oranges, mangoes and papaya he's brought from North End road market.
Harini… What do you think of Harini, huh?
Mmmn… a bit Hare-krishna. But certainly apt! She came in a hurry!
Mum doesn't get his joke she is so spaced out. She hasn't eaten since breakfast yesterday.
So, mmn… you don't like Harini? Then how about… Piyara? Or maybe a goddess name… like Parvati…?

Whatever you want, his gruff reply pierces her cloud.

You're the one who wanted children. I didn't.

Mum heard him then. Her yearning for papaya was gone. What Papa said to her the day after I was born stuck in her throat.

So, when my brother arrived months after Mum had left our Papa, she called him Krishna to be perverse. Luckily without the Hari. Papa didn't argue with her naming me Parvati. He wanted thundering, powerful females near him.

Now we don't even know where our Papa is? The last we heard of him he had 'gone native' on the Solomon Islands because he looked uncannily like one of the Warriors they still pray to on the smaller islands.

The evening *Swami-Ji* leaves for Bihar we go to prayers after *Bhajans. Swami-Ji* puts blessed ash on our forehead and gives me a mantra, which I'm forbidden to reveal. *Swami-Ji* wants to join us up with Mum. She has promised she will speak to her friend at the British Embassy in Delhi to do something about us. She says under her breath that it is an *Outrage!*

I reply, 'Yes *Swami-Ji*. I'd really, really like you to help. Please?'

She holds my gaze and nods gravely. 'I know you do, my love.'

Krishna tries to copy me. But burbles 'Yes-thank-you-Mum-but-don't-ever-leave-us-because-I-love-you-Mummy!'

He jabbers so fast that *Swami-Ji* doesn't realise it's like a prayer for Mum. Or did the dickhead imagine that *Swami Lalleshwari* is our Mum come back with blue eyes?

Swami-Ji does not laugh: her eyes fill up as she walks us through the crowd. Putting a hand each on our shoulders, she clears a path through the temple where people are chanting, waiting, praying. We get clear of the stifling, incense-soaked air to where the sun has just set, leaving a *seenimuthu* pink sky. I'm aware our *Swami* friend grows taller like a magic genie each time we see her. She clasps workmanlike hands on my shoulder and on Krishna, leading us to the two cupolas, she turns to face the *Vimana* while she looks outward to the fierce, unruly waves.

My ears stop hearing the words she speaks. Her mouth is moving, but there is no sound: I shake my fingers in my ears and my hearing clears. In a softer voice, she seems to be talking to herself.

'…are special children. Very blessed young people. The reason you were sent here is not clear to you now. One day when you are far from here—and you *will* be, dudes. You'll know it was some kind of—like your training with Footy, Krishna? Don't take this as a punishment. It's simply a process, chum. Understand?'

A shiver runs down my body. *Swami-Ji* holds my chin in her palm so I gaze into the ocean of her eyes. Not the turbulent grey sea we are forbidden to swim in, but an indigo, nurturing sea of hope.

'Yes, loud and clear!' some cartoon character voice escapes Brat.

My throat locks. I'm so afraid I might burst into sobs. I can't believe our *Swami-Ji* is going from us. We can't stop her. We can't go with her.

From a woven purse *Swami-Ji* extracts a leaf and pops it under my tongue; she does the same for Brat.

'Don't chew, it's Holy Tulsi' she murmurs.
When I look at her mouth it is not moving. Yet I can
hear her speak….

You are named after the fierce and powerful
Goddess, remember Parvati. You are the incarnation of
her and you're in this world to be a warrior. Fear
nothing and nobody. In the Puranas, Parvati performed
a penance to marry Shiva, a celibate bramachari. We
all have to pay in our own way. You may be paying
some price now…but never worry, you will sit astride a
tiger and fear no mortal!

Her words seem to melt into my burning chest.
A grumpy temple *Swami* in brown robes appears out of
nowhere with a group of ashram dignitaries, all high
and mighty. They look apprehensive; as if they think
Swami-Ji may not want to leave us here, so they form a
circle and slowly usher our friend towards the sandy
courtyard where the dusty chappals are left in rows.

Devotees are draping garlands of marigolds
they have strung into chains to dangle down the white
Oxford Ambassador, like to decorate wedding cars.
Seeing that white car waiting for *Swami-Ji*—the only
person able to connect us to Mum—makes me want to
hide in the boot. I'm sure the same thought has
occurred to my brother.

Swami-Ji descends the steps in bare feet
followed by a worried looking gaggle of
Brahmacharini in flimsy white saris, looking excitable,
ready to catch a bride's bouquet. *Swami-Ji* slides easily
into the marigold-festooned Ambassador and winds her
window down.

I try to move. I try to catch her eye.

The bad-tempered *Swami* who won't usually allow us to stand here, sees me and today he looks right through us!

Neither my brother nor I can leave the spot.

Maybe *Swami-Ji* has turned us invisible?

Has she rooted us to the earth?

We watch the flower-decked car start up and carry our friend away. I don't know how long we stand like pillars. Nobody dares to shoo us away.

Is this the effect of her Mantra?

I could swear something has changed. Suddenly, here at the edge of the Indian Ocean, so far from home—where Mum grew strawberries, purple cauliflowers and prize peas for our local Corsley farmers Show—I don't feel abandoned anymore.

I'm not sure how long I can keep my mantra a secret, or how I stop myself strangling the most irritating Brat on this planet, but I know one thing.

I will not let on how I make my curd so creamy.

SAM ALONE

My sweet Sam, I wish I knew where you've got to?

I have a recurring dream where I'm searching for you. I wake, then remember that I still don't even know your real name?

When I hear a hammering of piano scales by relentless fingers, smell Eucalyptus sap wafting on damp air or taste a mouthful of cream, I am back at The Darling Home…

I don't remember the godparents who emigrated to Australia the week after my Christening. Yet they came up trumps encouraging Ma to emigrate to Melbourne eight years later, acting as our sponsors. I was overjoyed that we were to meet these good fairies who sent birthday and Christmas pressies from afar. *The Keep Australia White Policy* was in place (not that I knew what it meant) but Ned and Barbara - light-skinned Burghers – had been welcomed.

Ma had felt assured with Irish roots and English mother-tongue, she wouldn't need to sit the notorious 'Test' to prove we were *white* enough to qualify. At our final interview at the Australian Consulate of Colombo *to inspect the accompanying child*—her cherished dreams were smashed.

Ma passed the Test; I did not.

Shipping companies were warned not to issue tickets to those unlikely to get through. But Ma had fallen prey to middle-men who trade on the desperate ones. I was sent to an orphanage in the hills so my single mother could work as school Matron to recoup emigration costs. It confused us to hear—through cousins in England—that £10 Assisted Passages to Australia were being handed out by the same body who kept us from getting in!

The painful blow to Ma was losing face: I notice how she niftily fobs off inquisitive relatives inquiring why we were spurned at the last stile. It irks her to admit—to Barbara and Ned— their goddaughter is a shade too dark to enter their new world.

The following year Australia's new government abolishes this notorious law. Younger Australians, bashful about a policy blatantly named 'Keep Australia White' start calling it the *White Australia Policy*. Their embarrassment does little to alter *your* life turning upside down, Sam? Mere months after you get ditched here on your own, this preposterous law is scrapped, too late! The rest of your family of nine sail to Brisbane without even leaving their address.

Life at the Darling Home goes on a pace.

No time for settling in. We have to grasp the torch and run. Everyone is bolting to town with farm produce, some were racing to Walters Meadow to cram in the afternoon milking shift. If the human dynamo Eva Darling finds her 'duckies' slowing she bellows in peculiar English phrases:

No slacking, ducks!

On with yer seven league boots, mes amis!

That's more like it, now you have the bit between your teeth...

Did we understand what she meant?

It was not civil servant English drilled into me by bottle-blonde Miss Jansz in Kirillipona, where Ma scraped her rupees to guarantee whatever else we lack, that I was well-spoken. The rough boys at this place have not heard anything like it, they hoot at my pronunciation. Now there is too much to get accustomed to in my first weeks without having to decipher this strange Englishwoman's odd commands.

Our local market town has been dubbed Little England because of its quaint British reminders: a racecourse and stables, a man-made lake to mimic a Loch, a Grand Hotel in mock-Tudor style—once the home of British Governor, Sir Edward Barnes. We learn in History that our locale was so favoured by Nile explorer, Samuel Baker. He imported a Blacksmith with an entire Forge and even a herd of Hereford cattle for his rural retreat. Since then it has developed into a hill-resort when the hot season drives city folk from the plains.

Ma and I first set eyes on Eva Darling when we got lost while camping with friends. We fetched up at her Children's Home instead. Now here I am, tagging onto her blue-eyed troupe while Mrs Darling directs her fruit-picking duckies with military precision.

Risking a shortcut through the golf course was a small miracle when the Darling woman offered Ma an instant solution to her pressing problem. My aunts who allow us a few nights stay at either end of the holidays are stupefied when Ma finally admits I'm going to join *tea-bush babies*!

Ma is letting the side down, they scold. I'm sad not to see my Colombo cousins like I do once a year. Yet I know my mother prefers me out of the way.

I'm initially confused at these pale-skinned Eurasian waifs with rosy-cheeks and sing-song accents. Then I catch sight of your vibrant face, Sam, eyes like tamarind seeds, teeth like sea shells filling your cheeky smile. I am hopeful I've spotted another one like myself. The feeling that I'm being punished for being the wrong colour soon fades.

Unlike us newbies, the girls here have nimble fingers—taking after their tea-picker mothers who learnt to select two-leaves-and-a-bud at early apprenticeship. You and I are given easy jobs—fetching and tidying after the older boys harvesting the pears and local peaches. Even the tiniest boys fearlessly scale Ragalla apple trees. Many have been left here as small babies. They wheel the barrows to the bottom of our rugged hill to load onto lorries. There's no road beyond this dead end, just hard red earth sluiced into ruts by ferocious rains that wash down Mount Pedro, the island's highest peak.

No surprise that the outside world leaves these small solemn outcasts alone.

What better spot to hide a shoal of fair-haired, mixed-bloods with mountain-goat feet? None of them wear shoes, despite the frosty climate. Their determination and stamina come from hardy Scots and Irish roots— the pioneering grandfathers of these barefoot children cleared the forests to tame into tea estates they named Somerset, Dalglish, Connemara, Strathspey. Those entrepreneurs ingeniously turned a disastrous Coffee Blight around to give birth to a new industry. Tea. When tea Planters get forced out of the island their progeny - *tea bush babies* are left stranded. Our benefactress knew how vulnerable they were. Without her Home to corral them in relative safety, Eurasian babies of native women and foreign men can end up as domestic servants in rich people's houses; sometimes, it's muttered, even worse.

I was too young to understand what that meant.

Mrs Darling is bent on educating her duckies so they won't be aliens in their own land. Britain was unaware they exist. In Sri Lanka they are considered Foreign. She forms a choir to train her duckies to belt out The Hallelujah Chorus. The farm which was set up by her missionary Grandfather feeds the colony, providing life skills for the boys. Produce like strawberries, lettuce and herbs go straight to the hotels. Many of these youngsters arrived with no birth certificates, just a pencilled scrap of paper relinquishing responsibility, signed with a thumbprint. They have no name of mother. And the name of their white father is kept under lock and key—if known at all.

One glance at your lively eyes and I know you have been part of a family who gave you birthday parties and picnics. Unlike these orphans you, Sam, have been cuddled, embraced and loved.

Optimism exudes from under your long eyelashes at eight years old. I, two years older, know I don't belong in this place either.

How did your family tell you they were leaving you?

Did they say they would never return when they left on that ship for Brisbane?

It is your brilliant idea to share my trunk of clothes with our tattily garbed mates. With no possessions, they rely on donations from the Red Cross. Remember that musty box- room we called Wardrobe? It smelt of wet dog and camphor balls. Our friends line up for Mary-*Akka* to issue their week's ration; one navy gymslip, shrunken Cardi or moth-eaten kilt—plus two pairs of scratchy woollen knickers. You arrived ahead of me, bagging the biggest locker. While helping me unpack you spot a flared polka dot skirt: your aunt had sewn you a dress in the same cloth, you told me, hugging it like a favourite teddy. I let you borrow my skirt until the next visit from the *dhobi* and so begins a trend. My white-elephant trunk becomes a success with the duckies. I may have alienated myself with too many hand-stitched frocks till you hit on that nifty solution.

Your bright eyes and curls lead to your nickname of Sambo from this barefoot tribe. You don't go looking for unkindness, so your irrepressible sense of fun soon makes you their mascot. Their view of the world is filtered through the time-warped collection of dog-eared books from an era of Edward Lear, Mervyn Peake, Kipling and Dr Seuss. Yet the stories that really grab us are dusty volumes of a hard-bound *Strand Magazine*.

Its small text pages punctuated with black and white illustrations of Eva Darling's fearless compatriots in Victorian garb, having daring adventures in far-flung territories.

Here, in the shadow of the highest peak—Pidurutalagala—surrounded by eucalyptus forests, icy streams, bear, sloth and wild boar, we are isolated. Once in a while, a lone mountaineer out trekking may descend in the wrong direction, bolting downhill with panicked eyes, as if he were being chased by the man-eating leopard of Punyanai. One of the boys returning from the early milking round might point him toward the Trout Farm, just as astonished to see an outsider. Every year the big guys go through an initiation, led by the staunchest Brit 'year-men' to climb that treacherous mountain at dawn. They are sworn to secrecy, fat leeches bulging from the top of their socks like drunken maggots.

During the school holidays, the children work on the fruit farm to earn pocket money—milking or picking berries. Even the youngest take turns cleaning lavatories, outside drains, with big girls on kitchen duties. I grab the coveted job—churning cream from our Jersey herd into butter because I enjoy collecting the cream at Kitchen House cooling in a vat. I have to skim it into a bowl to deliver to the fridge in Staff House where it is added to each day, then churned into butter. There are nifty shortcuts between Houses on this rugged hill; I learn which ones are too perilous for the staff to manage. Only you clock my wickedness: your sideways smile when you spot my tell-tale smears says you know where I've been!

The orphanage, despite its senseless rules, is the first safe harbour of my rolling-stone life since we got turfed out of our home when Ma committed a shameful sin. You and I commandeer the damp-smelling Wardrobe for a nook so I can relay plots from English films; *Ben-Hur, Spartacus* and *Jail House Rock*.

Yet, these innocent toughies remain suspicious of a city child wearing shoes. One way to drill into their solemn hearts is to demonstrate dance sequences from the Cliff Richards film.

Why do I try so hard with these stateless children whom nobody wants?

Perhaps it makes me feel less hard-done-by?

I didn't have a clue that Margie can't remember what her mother looks like: or Vimala was separated from the sister; that Elsie, abandoned age three, is unaware the tearful, shamefaced, Sinhala woman who visits her once a year, is related! Elsie sighs after she's left 'Oh, my parents send their servant with my pocket money because they've gone abroad'.

The older girls are tactful not to let on that 'the servant' *is* her mother.

I could never have guessed how you had been cruelly severed from your family. There were questions I dared not ask—why they had to choose the only orphanage on the island intended *for white kids*? Yet you never complain, not even about the harsh weather. You do not whinge when you get stuck in a makeshift sickroom because the Polio epidemic shuts down the whole place; or raise a fuss at a thrashing from our hated teacher the older boys call Sloth. You have a talent to blend in.

Our quirky grand dame pokes her head out of Staff House to holler *Now move it ducks or I'll have yer guts fer garters!*

You knew in a flash she meant we better beat it to the chapel down the hill.

Your two-thousand-watt smile warms me through and through on frosty mornings when we gather round that urn to sip scalding black tea before getting stuck into morning chores. For me, Sam equals sunshine! Yours is the most infectious grin. As if you couldn't wait to tell me some astonishing secret. It gets me out of bed in a joyful mood.

I wonder where you are, Sam?

When the rest of us feel we are dealt a dud card, you alone embrace that unforgiving world, perched on a cloud mountain, distilled by Tea-country in a wilderness unmarked on any map.

And you'd never dream of stealing the cream.

PARADISE ROAD II

There are no verandas to let the breeze in. None anywhere. These windows are built for a cold country. The smell inside Mignon's mansion is strange. Beyond the heady whiff of wax polish and orchids there is something else... it stifles me. Makes me still. I can only take short, shallow breaths inside this house. When I am allowed out, I can breathe again. The minute Mignon sweeps Selma upstairs to show her 'things of no interest to a child' I creep out of the heavy double door with brass fittings kept shut through the day.

Under the portico is another planet. The air is soft with the normal noises of birds in the jungle shrubbery, where giant millipedes assure me, I am still part of the world. An endless source of comings and goings in the anthill keep me fascinated. Here, in a Jam-fruit tree thousands of ants build their fortress. From a safe distance on the parapet, I watch rapt though fearful as the armies go about.

Yet I am more afraid of what Mignon will do to us. No people call at this grand Casa Bianca, but stranger is the lack of tradesmen; no malu-man swings his Ping-yo shoulder basket of *parau* and mullet from the dawn fish auction; no paper boy on a bike, no knife sharpener wielding his sharpening tool—like half a Singer sewing machine.

Saddest, no pedlar man with a trunk of goodies to offer the domestics cheap treats; a reel of bright cotton, combs of rough coconut shell, handmade ornaments or Indian hair oil in tiny bottles. And how do they manage without the travelling barber—a circus act with the flick of his pointed scissors at speed, yet never snipping an ear? Although I remember once, a pavement barber accidentally cutting the outer edge of someone's ear; the cure was instant and miraculous. The barber plucked a cobweb from the corner of the nearest shop doorway like a magician to wind over the tiny wound. Stops bleeding. Makes the onlookers cheer.

One minute we had not even known Mignon, the next she sailed into our lives so we're on this isolated estate, surrounded by a high brick wall in a tightly shut up house of many rooms.

Each day she commandeers more chunks of Selma's time. Mignon's shopping sprees take place in yet a different universe. Her lavish escapades may be some cruel game to encourage Selma to visit the Jesuit Father for catechism. Like my mother, I am spellbound when we are allowed to forage in this smart end of town.

Before Mignon came to our aid when Swine did the dirty on Selma, I hated the mention of shopping; being dragged around the Pettah Bazaar.

The honking car horns, the clatter of trams against the cobbled roads in the old quarter had my mother's nerves on edge long before she got bartering with the yelling mob of street vendors. In limited Sinhala she infuriated the man, told him he sold rubbish, called him a liar, walked off in pretence she didn't want the item, loitered long enough to be called back to offer a *final price*; now he had cut the cloth so she would have to give in. Pulling out crumpled notes, Selma counted them, keeping her gaze in the opposite direction. This pantomime with screaming hawkers amidst pyramids of bright cloth would lead to one of her headaches.

Only then would she give up the fight and limp off with blistered feet to take refuge in a tea house or ice-cream parlour; anywhere with a working fan. Here, over lukewarm ginger beer we recovered from blaring heat and inspected the 'bargain.' These establishments were not chosen for hygiene, my mother never failed to remind me. I had to drink with a straw. If a visit to the bathroom was needed her face would say 'don't-even-ask!'

I was essential to those trips whatever town we happened to be homeless in, when Selma discovered my inborn talent for locating a correct bus to get us home. Long after the beggars' have pawed at us in the bus terminus with deformed or mutilated babies thrust in our faces, jostled and shoved, we would get back drenched in perspiration, arms lifeless from carrying bundles of fabric purchased for a song. I used to dread this responsibility thanks to my compass for finding the way home, but how odd that now I miss that: being an essential tool to my mother? And I'm almost missing those five sweet months when the Swine and Selma were 'a couple'.

After they fell adrift, ashamed of being thwarted and her nest-egg ripped off, Selma made me swear I'd never mention that unfortunate episode.

Shopping with the Grand Dame allows Selma and me into a rarefied world.

Mignon did not equip her cream mansion by scavenging discounted cloth in dusty Pettah markets. I heard her rubbing it into my impoverished Selma how she missed shopping in Rome's Via Condotti, in exclusive corridors in Florence, plush arcades of Jermyn Street when they stayed with Quintus's father near Hyde Park. Accompanying her to Colombo merchants she favours, we barely step inside the emporiums when tea is brought on lacquer trays; sweetmeats wrapped in edible silver leaf are proffered. If Madame desired something cool a boy was dispatched to Pagoda Tea rooms and what about a chocolate ice for the young lady? Extra fans are wheeled into the inner sanctum for the big spender, while a team of cream-shirted relatives of the proprietor unravel Vietnamese brocades, fretted silk from Burma, Shantungs and silk chiffon with recklessness.

It uses all my self-control to resist flinging my shoes off and playing leap frog over the wondrous ribbons of gem-colours. In my ideal world this is all I want to eat; colours! Selma, sitting daintily beside her friend,is out of her depth. I perch on the sofas and watch, eagerly stuffing away pistachio pastries no one else has time for. My poor mother is suspicious of a shopkeeper who'd give anything for free (was she this weird before Swine?) so her hauteur verges on rudeness.

While Mignon talks in a low throttle, Selma sends the retainer back and forth for substitute brews. Oh no… lime cordial is too sharp, iced coffee too sweet and when the drinks are finally perfect, she waits till I aim a yummy sweetmeat at my mouth to shake her head in disgust.

'No, no! You don't know how long that sat out attracting flies…'

She mellows, after cool glances from her friend. In time she finds how to parade a passable act as lady-of-leisure perusing exorbitant trinkets, knowing the less she says the better. Selma's mood changes from incredulity, watching her friend part with piles of notes for intricate beaded handbags with matching accessories—the seed pearls hand stitched by women in purdah. This is interspersed with banter along the lines '…or shall we look somewhere else before you make your final choice dear?'

Realising Mignon knows this to be the best dealer in Kashmiri shawls so fine one could be passed through a wedding ring - she has to belt up. Yet within two seconds of the transaction completed, Selma comes to respect that object of Mignon's desire—even if she had just attempted to steer her from buying it. Now she's humbled by Mignon's new toy, bowed in defeat. It makes me sad to watch her acting so reverent to its new owner.

The biggest blow is when I realise that Selma is so under the fiend's spell that she has backed off from our visit to my Uncle Muldoon. The only Uncle I treasure from Selma's vast family! We have looked forward to this mad fortnight in the Badulla hills. There is no place Selma can let her hair down for a rollicking good time.

My cousin Amari and I stay awake past midnight telling ghost stories while the adults play poker. No banalities like bedtimes exist in that household. We accompany Uncle Muldoon to the tennis Club in get-ups borrowed from Aunty Nellie's fancy almirah, looking like harlots from the 1940s. For years I thought Clemi, my older cousin had called us 'Charlottes'. The only time Selma has been happy is with her best loved brother she calls Mul (the Sinhala word for Flower). It sets us up for the rest of the year's wanderings. I can't believe she'd give up this vital 'medicine' for some idiotic party of Mignon's.

On the backseat of the Chevrolet, I retreat into my book: Celeste has escaped from the men in the Fez hats to rescue the lost statue from the tomb. Today the Fort pavements are under shadow as Mignon parks in front of the recently built Ceylenco building. It was the first public building to boast an escalator. For the initial months after it opened, people poured off the streets to experience this new adventure. Going up a staircase without moving your feet! The new thing from the West. Selma is under the rich witch's spell. They leave me in the car and trot towards the BOAC building, carting a well-stuffed briefcase. I idly clean my ear with a finger nail, gaping through the window, watching a parrot-green Peugeot colliding with a bare-chested rickshaw coolie.

It is not the rickshaw man's fault yet the driver gets out and yells abuse at the injured coolie. In moments, passersby dawdle to aid and abet. The man is bleeding from his head while the driver is threatening him.

I have observed it so many times, but perhaps because I'm sitting in a smart car, I feel disgusted with the busybodies siding with the driver when they had not witnessed it. The woman and small boy passengers walk off without paying. I long to leap out and administer First Aid like Nurse Celeste would have. The rickshaw coolie is resigned to his miserable fate. Is that how Selma and I must appear to other people? So pitiable that they are forced to let us scrounge a bed for a week of the school holidays?

Mignon's large frame suddenly appears at my window, giving me a jump. She wriggles in and starts up the air-con while reaching for her driving shoes.

'Did you see? It was the driver's fault…' I gasp, unafraid of Princess Rhino for once.

She is smiling to herself, in another dimension, too distracted to notice the fuss on the opposite pavement.

'They don't look where they're going. Probably the coolie was drunk…'

'Can't we stop at the police station and report it?' I ask. My mother joins us, merry.

Mignon says cooly, 'Alright now, Florence Nightingale, can you watch your side and tell me how much room there is?' before reversing the car.

Mignon licks her lips, revs the motor and sails off past the Old Continental Hotel. My battered rickshaw man is left like a crumpled sparrow on the pavement, surrounded by crows about to peck him to pieces.

'Hah!' she lets out a satisfied sigh which sounds like a cat's fart. 'That…. is what I call a lucrative morning's work!'

'I don't know how you do it!'

'We have Queenie to thank for alerting me to the *annus mirabilis*.'

Mignon steers round the House of Parliament roundabout onto the Galle Road; we have the sea to our right, passing the Galle Face Green.

I realise how much I've missed the stroll we often made after choir practise at our Anglican church. It was a spot where Swine often loitered in his borrowed automobile to whizz us to the Fountain Café for an ice cream sundae. All these weeks at Casa Bianca and not once have we been out in the evening. I thought about that injured rickshaw man and wondered if he were dead?

'This must go like clockwork—no trembling knees at the eleventh hour!'

'Course not, I gave you my word, no?'

'You'll have to stay until this is *fait accomplis, sil vous plait...* '

Selma is hesitant; like she can't understand the French.

'Er... I thought you said they won't have availability for two months?'

'So?' The hawk nose is indignant. Now the jowls begin working away. 'What should that matter?'

'Ah—I have to put Missie to the boarding?'

I cannot see my mother's face from where I sink down on the back seat to feign sleep, but I can feel Mignon's agitation. As we reach the environs of our gilded prison at Casa Bianca, she slows the car to a crawl.

'So how d'you think he will co-operate if you've gone off into the blue? Sometimes I wonder if you understand the seriousness....'

'No, no I won't let you down...'

'—expect me to wait another ten years for… a cripple to die?' she spits in a hoarse whisper as we get in sight of the outer walls. Her jowls work overtime like a volcano laid dormant while brewing its wickedness.

Selma pacifies her 'You can count on me!'

'….has seen to it that I don't get a red cent when… all is written to his son and heir.'

She beeps impatiently for the boy to open the gates so I only catch bits '…rent it out to an embassy …escape this dead end!"

I manufacture a credible yawn and stretch to arise from my snooze.

'Ah look? Sleeping Beauty won't be sleeping much tonight…'

But I was day-dreaming of Iggy. I wish he'd come back as suddenly as he did that evening on his scooter down the drive. I was under the Jesuit Father's spell. Why Mignon dragged my mother to secret sessions in his monastery yet wouldn't let me even snatch a glimpse of him, while I was made to wait in the car week after week, was an unknown question: why Mignon calls the priest 'Father' in front of Quintus, when Quintus clearly knew him well enough to call him Iggy so fondly. When speaking with Selma she lapses into saying Iggy…

I will never make a good detective. Why do grown-ups have to be so round-the-corner-behind-the-bush?

On the morning of my tenth birthday, arrangements from the silent core of seven or eight houseboys become brisker.

I feel ashamed they have extra work on account of 'my' party Mignon dreamt up without even asking Selma? Or me? The ants, my only friends, muster. Deep in that anthill under the huge tree they pick up the vibrations from the house. They must have sent off invitations to far-off relatives saying, rich pickings afoot.

The ants gather in parades three deep. Alongside Mignon's wordless slaves hurrying on bare feet to move chairs and tables, polish furniture, these minute torturers are steadily building their own city. I detect a super-species of Colonel-in-Chief ants; smaller than the giant rust-coloured variety. To make sure everyone knows them, they sport an extra bump on the head. Perhaps that is what held the poison to swell your tongue and choke you?

Mignon must carry her poison concealed inside her chignon?

I am in awe of the preparations but fear none of the school mates she has asked from Mountcastle school in Campbell Place will find their way here. The huge thrill is when the dark green Elephant House Morris Minor van turns down the long drive to deliver a mysterious white box— instantly secreted away—but I was allowed to peep at the party breads in green, yellow and red for sandwiches. Something I've only seen in foreign magazines. And then, I gasp when I spot a whole wooden crate of Coca Cola! My school chums would not believe *we have Coca Cola,* it was so utterly new from abroad. A girl whose father works in an embassy claimed she'd tasted this wine-coloured stuff in a curvy bottle which the adults use as a 'mixer'. Nobody wasted it on children. I scuttle up the bitter chocolate stairway to deliver this newsflash to Selma in the old gent's study, massaging his bad shoulder.

Just having my mother nearby makes Quintus chuckle. Even though Selma is well up on imported goods, Coca Cola has not registered on her radar.

'Uncle Quintus, a very important question. Have you tasted Coca Cola?'

'Coja Cola? Oooh, give me a clue—no, can't say I have…' he is merrier now Selma has told him she is staying on longer.

'A kind of cider, isn't it? Like Perry-ade?' Selma is clueless.

'Well, we had Barq's Root beer on that voyage to New York. Now there's one herbal tonic I can vouch for! Barq's puts hairs on your chest. Ahar!'

'Oh yuck! Was that before Coca Cola was invented?'

For one brief moment I buckle under and believe I've been too hard on Mignon. Why is she going to the expense of buying Coca Cola for a kid's party?

I skip downstairs and my mouth hangs open at the transformation of the stuffy mansion with streamers and bunches of balloons. Mignon stands directly under the chandelier giving instructions that the Cola is to be kept solely for adult consumption. Mustering what little bravado is left, I pirouette to show her the dress she insisted on purchasing in a Chatham Street shop, with blue ankle socks to match the Chinese trimmings. Chief Purser scrutinises my outfit like I'm a Humpty she is thinking of upholstering. Her face has an expression like she is sniffing to detect mould.

Then Mignon twitches to dispatch me to locate a can-can petticoat; to apply whitener to my shoes; to powder my face.

Blooming ugly witch with pox-marked jowls d'you think I want a face like you?

I trudge upstairs feeling one hundred and ten years old. I have no enthusiasm for this gathering. I fervently wish they'd all stay home.

Selma douses me in splashes of her new bottle of Balenciaga Cologne and slaps a feathery powder puff on my cheeks, causing me to splutter.

'Don't tear open the presents in front of people—close your mouth—keep them for later alright?'

'Mmnn, enough! …so do we get to Uncle Mul's place?'

Selma has returned to touching up her already made-up lips with a swirl of Majorca Sunrise. She sighs.

'Can't go anywhere till Quintus is deposited to the Up-Country joint.' She looks in the mirror as if giving herself a talking-to. 'Can't budge before that's taken care of.'

'Then can we go?'

'Then we can go to Timbuktu!' Selma's frown clears.

I'd not heard of Timbuktu; it sounds like it may be close to Trincomalee, which I *do* remember well, if only for the jellyfish that are so devilish, they are known as Men of War and you'll be mad to go near one. I hope it has a lagoon in this Timbuktu place? I don't know whose house is there.

The invitation said 5pm. Soon after 4.30 a stream of cars creep down the drive—like a funeral procession, really slow—as if they planned to arrive together. Within minutes the solitude of Case Bianca is enlivened by squeals from a dozen girls, some older sisters and random adults looking uncertain whether to enter through the main door.

I do not recognise any adults amongst a small cloud of ladies strutting in afternoon sarees of orchid, canna pink, mint green, but you can tell they are in awe of this palazzo.

Our Chatelaine in cream shantung two-piece, flapping obediently at her thick white calves, is trying to appear friendly. Her chignon is piled even higher with all the venom she is hoarding; being pleasant does not come naturally to Mignon. But for some reason, today she is desperate to act like a normal person.

Veeramani and sister Suzanthi, girls whom I've known since our mums were old friends, lope arms and rescue me from my receiving post, conspirators in a second.

'So, what's with this big party then?'

'What have you done to get such a show?' Vee yanks me behind a pillar.

'You haven't come of age, have you?'

'Are you mad? I need a bit more time. She is trying to impress…. Father Ignatius.'

'Amma told us about the Jesuit!' Suzanthi's eyes are smouldering.

Vee, who is fourteen but taller than her sister, peeps over the heads of the arrivals 'Is he here yet?'

'He looks better tha…' I cast my eyes heavenward, feeling important for the first time. '…better than *Fabien*!'

They open their mouths in a silent scream of yearning.

'*Ane*! How come *you* get to stay in this film set of a house? I'm jaaaay!'

'True, like Fabien? Let's meet him,' sighs the older, looking more like Aunty Ena than before.

'She's laid on a show fit for a Twenty-First do, ah? I wonder what she is wanting back from your mother?' Vee looks enviously at the centrepiece—a plain iced cake with no writing on.

I can't stop the grin contorting my face. These girls knew about handsome men. Their brother—a cricketer, renowned for his good looks—died last year, aged nineteen, crashing off a practice bar in the garage. Aunty Ena turned white-haired within three months. She began wearing white when her doctor husband died years back; now her platinum hair and white saree gives her a new glamour. She was the only Burgher friend Selma knows to adopt the saree, but she's revelled in her connection with a man of native birth. He had been a Colombo surgeon who looked a twin of Bandaranaike, our Prime Minister who was gunned down by a Buddhist monk.

Ena is perfectly at ease with Quintus in the dining room where a couple of dads and teenage boys are clustered round a mirror-topped table. Decanters of whisky, gin and White Arrack stand with the cherished new Coca Cola. Despite Casa Bianca being a European household, the males present are still shy to mix with the ladies so lurk by Quintus in his wheelchair, not daring to stray from the invisible fence. This daft segregation was a sore point with Selma when we went to funerals or weddings where women and men sat separately. Today it becomes useful for Selma to gate-crash the 'male parlour' to chit-chat with Ena knowing Mignon won't come anywhere near her Enemy.

Only Father Ignatius mixes freely among the fluff on the terrace where cheese straws, asparagus rolls and miniature Elephant House eclairs are passed over for the Dish of the Day in his party frock—a black cassock with a heavy cross almost reaching his waist.

84

The treasure hunt and tiresome games Mignon made my mother organise are designed to get us hot and cross.

Fancy buying imported apples (at Cargills) strung from the dwarf Guava trees, expecting 10 and 11-year-old girls with hands tied behind their backs to jump up and munch them? It was a game for tiny boys. While leading the troops on the treasure hunt, I catch glimpses of brisk looks between Aunty Ena and Selma, walking her friend round the back door; Ena's driver loading up large carrier bags of 'sewing'. I am either gasping for breath or mopping off the sweat. However, when Vee and Suzanthi join us for Sardines it's giggles all the way.

At last, this damp squib of a party ends. I stand beside the trolley where Mignon made me pile the tower of birthday presents, running my fingers along the smooth ribbons. I have little urge to unwrap them. Even the iced Elephant House centre-piece admired by the scented ladies, remains un-cut and un-loved - like Casa Bianca. Boss Woman chose a date cake! None of the youngsters would have eaten that?

Iggy seems eager to try it. I cut him a slice large for his Jesuit-mates, wrapping it in two paper napkins; then seeing Mignon is not about, I grab a cream damask serviette from the sideboard. Father Ignatius looks like a boy caught doing something naughty as he stuffs it into the depths of his cassock.

'I almost forgot…' He reaches into his seemingly bottomless garment to reveal a matchbox. It has no wrapping. I slide it open to see the tiniest amber beads.

'I had it blessed by Senor Don Evaristus. He was passing through from Lisbon'

A small rosary rose up on my finger, the links between the beads practically invisible. I can't think of a thing to say but my temples throb like a drum and a voice inside my chest is hammering. Why am I terror-stricken that I may never see him again?

I try to speak above the din in my ears. 'Is it meant to keep me safe?'

Father Iggy nods solemnly, as if he now has a worrying thought.

'Indeed. I hope it will, child. Portugal is where our Order of Jesuits first originated, did you know? No, why should you…'

'Did the Portuguese bring their priests when they governed us?'

'They brought Catholicism—its why so many Catholic churches are on our west coast. Good question but no, the Jesuits did not reach our island till the end of the Dutch Period. They settled on the East coast and Jaffna where the Dutch did not have a stronghold. History does not always make sense, does it?'

Hearing the stiletto heels clicking down the corridor, he speedily draws a sign of the cross on my forehead, whispers something under his breath and turns.

'Thank you for coming, Father!' I call out to the empty space.

It is only then, with Vee, Suzanthi, Quintus and my mother, I get a chance to taste some of the Angels on Horseback and miniature playing cards in aspic, handmade to be the tiniest ace of Spades and Queen of Hearts. Aunty Ena joins us from the garden looking oddly flushed and as she closes the French windows against the encroaching mosquitos. I notice that Father Iggy is a long way down the drive, beside his scooter.

He is directing a garden boy at the gate on some important business.

I grab a half-filled glass from a tray that is being carried past. I pounce on the tepid coke and guzzle it. Why did I expect it to taste like Ginger beer? This is bitter-ish but intoxicating. The residue bubbles still manage to make me choke. I drag myself upstairs, not minding that I'd missed the chocolate éclairs, that I had not had Happy Birthday sung or tasted the cake.

Yes, I have tasted Coke Cola!

And I have a blessed necklace thingy all the way from Jesuit land. I may have fallen asleep in my clothes. In the middle of the night, Selma shakes me awake. At first, I think she is part of my dream because she is not speaking, just gesturing, urging me up. It is pitch-black outside; she leads me by the hand to the bathroom where the cool floor under my feet wakes me sufficiently to know this is no dream. I am so exhausted I feel like I am sleepwalking. Why is Selma fully dressed in the middle of the night? Why is she handing me day clothes instead of my nightie?

When I open my mouth she shushes me, keeping her voice in a whisper.

'Come quickly.' She peers from the bathroom window facing the drive, watching for someone.

I groggily pull clothes on, then realise the birds are starting their dawn chorus. Selma has no shoes on. She's ahead at the bedroom door, peering stealthily out of the room. I follow without question; a steady snore is the only sound. Selma checks the coast is clear, then doubles back to our room to pick up a small suitcase. In her other hand she carries her high-heels.

'Not a murmur!' She creeps towards the landing outside Mignon's room.

My heart is in my mouth. At the top of the stairs, she falters. I hold my breath and stay close, the brass balustrade faintly lighting our way. I take those steps down the carpeted stairs as if in a dream. I get ahead of Selma as we reach the ground floor and pull her in the direction of the breakfast room where a strand of dawn light creeps in.

I can almost hear a witch-voice calling, '*And where d'you think you're going without your insulation against the heat? Get some milk from the Coldrator!*'

Selma puts down her suitcase to unlock the tradesman's entrance with a key she takes from a ledge. There is no sound from the servant's quarters, but my heart thumps loud in my ears. I hear a squeak of brakes or is it the door creaking open? Selma bends to put on her shoes; she is taking too long. I think I understand what she was plotting with Aunty Ena. I grab the suitcase from her. It's heavier than expected. Is she stealing the family silver? In seconds we are over the threshold of Casa Bianca and onto gravel.

I feel brave. I don't care about the sharp stones underfoot. It's a long hike to the gate. I hug my shoes under my arm. How will my mother make it that far? Selma steers us to the left of the drive towards a screen of shrubbery, her hand on mine feeling like cold death. Twenty yards down the drive I urge her to run. She spots the black Morris Minor waiting round the rhododendron thicket; it free-wheels obligingly and my mother grabs the door with trembling hands. The driver is not even looking at us but hastily waves us in. He starts the engine and lets it purr in low gear toward the big gate which is unbelievably, already half-open for us.

I cling to Selma's arm and my heart is thumping like it is about to burst. Selma is rigid on the back seat. I can't breathe while the driver stops to get out and open the other half of the gate; as he enters the car again, I get the courage to peer back at Casa Bianca, outlined by a yellow back-light of dawn making it ghostly and beautiful.

At the very moment he turns onto the tarred road, an electric light gets switched on inside the house. It is in the very bedroom we have escaped from! Where I was fast asleep twenty minutes ago. My feet are solid blocks of ice. This must be what Mignon warned my mother about?

Selma never talks about our time in that gilded prison except in hushed whisperings to Aunty Nellie. I can't get answers to why we had to bolt without my birthday presents or what Mignon was forcing my mother into? It became a closed book.

I know Selma came close to doing something her conscience would not allow. By comparison, the embarrassment over Swine was small cheese, she can now laugh at that.

Mignon was never a laughing matter.

On an Up-Country train after what felt a century since escaping Casa Bianca, Selma spies a woman we think could be Mignon, much aged. We only glimpse her through two sets of dusty train windows, wearing large sunglasses, her big head relentlessly nodding. She looks hollow. All her venom leaked out, leaving the layers of maquillage hardened into a cracking mask. Selma and I take a sharp intake of breath at the same time. It looks like Mignon's grandmother – she has aged beyond recognition.

'Could it be really her?' I glare at my mother who has turned pale.

She mutters, '… Oh-my-god… if that's not Saint Vitus' dance, I'll eat my hat…'

'Saint *who?*'

'They have—er, another name for that illness nowadays… Oh merciful lord, that's what she's got…'

As the train screeches out from Talawakelle station, it takes the woman in a tailored dress out of our view, we sit still as statues.

Now Selma comes to life and explains who the charismatic Jesuit was. Father Ignatius, she later found, was Quintus' only son by his former wife, a Catholic-Tamil lady. Selma tells me it was Iggy who is rightful heir to Casa Bianca, had his calling permitted a Jesuit to own property.

When I stand up as the train slows for our station, I realise the years of fear for Mignon have stayed stuck onto my leatherette seat. I only feel pity for the fierce so-and-so who is shrivelled into a wreck.

FAST & LUCE

After a week of trawling for stock on the Welsh borders, I'm lazily content in my Dolphin Square hidey hole with brekky in bed. The dulcet tones of Quentin, my QC mate, nudge me awake from his chambers across the river. I admit Quentin gives good telephone, whatever time of day.

'Bit of business to take care of at Cholmondeley Hall. You've not seen it at Shooting Season, have you Luce?'

'I ain't bin at any season Guv, not considered of suf'cent importance'

'You'd enjoy smirking at Roald Lyttleton's newest Piece, who is among the party. And of course, Bradders is dying to see you again…'

'Mmn…I see. You don't mean *The* Roald Lyttleton?'

'Indeed. Art Crit at New Yorker! I'm uncertain how much we can trust that smooth-talking operator.'

'Who's driving?'

'Darling girl. Would I put my life in the hands of a mere mortal when it's - '

'Oh, shut up fuckface. I can't go anywhere with my roots in this state' I moan, remembering an overdue appointment with Charles.

'Your roots, Lucinda Frampton, are one of the significant things about you… don't change a hair…' Etcetera.

It will be humbling to brave my faded roots a tad longer. The attraction is none of these thoroughbreds Quentin tries to dangle; it is because he needs me. Or his silver-grey Bentley Continental '54 does. Takes me back to sitting in Daddy's lap driving around our Isle of Skye farm. One of my lasting memories before Daddy departed this world far too early. I'm glad Quentin had to give up driving after a hideous scare when they brought him back from the dead, twice in the same hour at Southmead General. It was a well-equipped spot to have an aneurism. Or he'd be up there with Daddy and the angels. Quentin is ace at finding the right location!

We rendezvous at the mews off Belgrave Square where he stables his vintage animal. I stash wellies and a niftily packed tote into the Bently's spotless boot and note the QC's luggage consists of two riding crops plus an entire crate, minus two bottles of Veuve Clicquot. How odd, since Quentin does not ride? I pretend not to notice them.

'Seems you're taking coals, Quentin?'

'Bradders owns the smartest Caviar Bar in Chester with sufficient champagne to fill his radiators. But deplete his stocks on mere weekend guests? Not a chance, babe!'

He uses words like 'babe'. the old sausage. Thinks it makes him sound youthful.

I belt up, lip and buckle, quickly checking eyebrows in the mirror for strays. 'You mean James Bradwick has become a mean arse?'

'You know these Bas Bleu have been long pillaging the locals, scrounging off their weekend guests. I come prepared…'

'Your clever habit saved us when we were caught out at that musty smelling pile in -'

'Oh, don't remind me of those sad parvenu'

'It put our friendship to the test Quentin -'

'Parading their shabby Moroccan rot gut, then for a treat, Elderberry wine brewed by the butler! I'm glad I had the foresight to keep supplies of that innocent little wine I picked up in Epernay in the boot.'

The Bentley effortlessly gobbles 156 miles of M1 and when we pass the cluster of oaks surrounding Bolsover Castle, a tickle of excitement reminds me this spot marks the start of the kingdom belonging to our host. We arrive at Cholmondeley Park ahead of the others. I need to reacquaint with James Bradwick. I have not glimpsed him since I was bridesmaid to his God-daughter, Savanna. Viscount Bradwick has a singularly forgettable face; he might pass for just about anyone but Heir to the 11th Duke of Warwick. This is what interbreeding brings.

'Lucindahhh!' James throws a bear hug to make me fear all life will be squeezed out. Yet he stops within centimetres of crushing my ribs like a well-trained hunting hound.

'You have not changed a days-worth, James. She must be very lovely?'

'Well, they say the love of a good woman contributes. Perhaps the love of a young woman is helpful to a chap's morale, eh?'

'Looks something of the sort. I'm longing to meet her.'

I try to divert his interest from where my sweater dress ends and leather boots begin. For the clan's benefit - Jamie has wed a pretty maid from Battersea whom nobody knows anything about. That should freshen up the genes. They were engaged within three months. Out popped the babies in quick succession so Bradwick is a happy chappie.

While Quentin wanders off to inspect the famed Temple - featured in a recently-aired historical TV series - Jamie quizzes me about my Portobello antique shop. I try to explain its name - Fast & Luce - without alarming him. Since my business partner Mathew Fast awaits trial in a Dallas prison, I don't want the tittle-tattles making out I'm in league with bad lads. When it comes to owners of important 'houses'- as we carelessly call our ancient palaces and moated Manors - it's as well to dot the i's and cross the t's. And write a real letter afterwards.

Funny how small things go a long way with this mob. It was my grandmama—her town house was in Grosvenor Square—who honed my up-bringing. The London home was papered from floor to ceiling in her Frazer Ancient Hunting plaid; even the wall-to-wall carpet was Tartan. I will never forget that place, which left me feeling dizzy, and I can't forget Granny's words.

'Lucinda dear, proper letters when thanking proper people! It's a rule you'll be grateful for one day.'

Accordingly, I never send anything less than a correctly worded snail mail with an actual stamp.

The Duchess of Stratton and Cheatham's connecting flight from Monte Carlo gets delayed and the Airport is 40 miles away, so dinner is put on hold. Roald Lyttleton sends a message that he is running late. This induces Quentin to uncork a brace of Bollinger (surprisingly provided by our host!) so when we lift handblown flutes in a toast to absent friends, we exchange a wink: may they be as absent as long as they please. It was delicious to prolong pre-dinner drinkies in one of the most pleasing noble homes I have visited in a while.

The only guest to arrive on time is the pert Essex-girl-made-good, Tat Evans, a scribe on one of the glossies. Tat is an avid teller of lies, yet I believe her when she claims she knew the Duchess while still plain Widdy Redford, a hirsute gal from Tasmania. After thawing out on her second glass, Tat reminds us Widdy was then a riotous circus act.

She initially married a political journo who worked long hours, leaving her free to widen her circle in Westminster. Widdy was dating and spanking three different MEPs. Her husband's framed photo was deftly slipped back into a drawer when he was out of the door. After the husband wises up and divorces Widdy, she, armed with connections, moves onto a retarded millionaire in need of regular thrashing.

Quentin adds how this very ordinary Tassa female set about conquering one of our few unwed Dukes in the kingdom.

'It didn't matter a jot that she talks like Edna Everage and walks like a camel with a bladder infection. Our gal from Hogsville, was out to collar a Coronet and we simply watched dumbfounded…'

Our host perks, excited at the mention of camels.

'God's truth Quentin! They are literally giving the luckless creatures away… Well, it beats s-s-s-slaughtering them in the outback. Completely ov-ov-overrun with these camels. So yes-es-es… for the price of transport alone, I am expecting delivery of three dozen rescued beasties very shortly.'

Viscount Bradwick seems overjoyed. Isn't it endearing when the wickedly rich get so thrilled about winning a freebie? He wants us to know the minutia of how you procure camels from the wastes of Central Australia, when faultlessly on cue, a noisy commotion erupts in the hall. A chilly wind off the North Pole is followed by Garibaldi announcing a guest who is lolloping into the drawing room.

'Her Grace… the Duchess of Stratton and…Ch-'

A broad antipodean voice soars over the butler's. I fear a helicopter has landed on the roof.

'Jeeez-zus! It's as dark as three feet up a crow's arse out there! What's the matter Brad, my ocker, trying to save yer lightbulbs?' thunders Her Grace, heaving a chummy embrace at James and finding a chair to park herself.

'…chess of Stratton and Cheatham' concludes Garibaldi, not moving a hair.

Quentin rises in salutation but we are too amazed by her entrance to move.

'Soo… who's a stoked batch of drongo's then?' She takes in the spent bottles from our first round, nostrils flaring.

Our eyes on stalks are dazzled by the headlights of her voracious stare. She fixes each of us as if we have price tags above our heads, deciding who is worth a Buckley's Chance.

'Been on a duck's dinner, have we luvvies? No drama—I made you's wait so you'll be ready to eat a horse, I bet? And chase the jockey!' Her Grace tries to look prim, as if banoffee pie wouldn't melt in her vast bucket of a mouth.

'As always, good things come to those who wait. And here, my dear. YOU. ARE!' lies our host so convincingly it brings out a deep guttural purr from Her Grace.

I can understand what makes this baby-faced Viscount such a natural Restaurateur, even if he passes for a lackey at his own gaff. He has that supreme quality to make any camel feel that she is Madonna.

Garibaldi hammers the dinner gong as if trying to teach us manners. James Bradwick leads us to a formal dining room on the upper floor of Cholmondeley, which may have been intimidating if not that we were nicely warmed by the pre-prandial, our host sighing 'sit where ye please!'

When you've already watched close-ups of your surroundings with actors playing Queen Victoria and Albert on these very dining chairs, it takes you into another dimension. Reality is briefly left behind. I single out the only male I don't yet know—Peter Rankin, a Maze designer—and plonk beside him. My legs are eighty percent Bolly and twenty percent jelly. I am, as Widdy noticed, famished enough to eat horsemeat, though the jockey may not be quite to my taste. Yet a woodcock on toast for first course slides down a treat. Peter's lion-eyes are up and down me, even though I have little doubt where his serious interests lie.

'Ah, so here's the great She-who-must-be-obeyed, his Lordship knows better as Strap'em and Beat'em?' Peter asks, as I lick my fingers of the last traces of the juicy bird.

'I hadn't heard that particular title?' I like his tapering finger tips. Artistic type. Impoverished, I don't doubt.

No sooner the next course— with a flamboyant pastry topping—has done a round, Widdy eases back her chair as if to make an escape.

Already?

'Excuse-I, dahlin's! Hafter go walkabout and see iffa can give birth to a politician - All that sitting in planes gives yer piles a verruca...'

Her Grace's excuse to powder her nose?

The men guffaw while two of them remember to stand, though it takes me three entire minutes to decipher her quaint colloquial.

Long after we have dallied with the cheese board and the Port is circulating in a ship's decanter, making me giddy simply to watch, James shoots up erect like he'd been stung by a bee. He is swerving from side to side as if he might be sick all over us; his arm reaches to grab the air, then wavers. He snatches a smouldering something being passed to him...

'No-no, h-h-hold on! Hold it! Its s-s-surely the wro- wro- wrong direction-' yelps our host, like a policeman at a country roundabout, directing traffic while carthorses hold sway.

Most of us are too flushed and drowsy to know what he means?

'Wait on! I d-d-d-don't think w-w-we are doing this correctly,' he wails, while Peter Rankin passes him another trumpet-shaped spliff.

———

'Yes, that's the thing to do, we must make it—Joint to the right, Port to the left, yah?'

'Correct form, Lordy!' Quentin swiftly assures, he understands these eccentrics and their querulous ways.

'If'ya don't mind me saying, yer Bogans…' Widdy has slipped in and is back on stage 'My dear hubby, the Duke explained correct etiquette you quaint English folk use to elbow the Port along when its hogged by some uncouth beggar... If only ah could remember what it wa-'

'You inquire about the Bishop's health, isn't that so?' Peter Rankin chirps eagerly, the new boy at school.

'One is meant say "*D'yo know the Bishop of Norwich?*"' our Viscount host is deadly serious.

'That's the ticket! Course, ah know that Bishop alright. Whipped him into shape on occasion. In diggery-doo land we don't stand on ceremony – we slug the yobbo an' grab the bottle!' Her Grace has a glazed expression. She seems to be conversing to someone far away. Is she communicating in psychic mode like indigenous tribes do at times of crisis or loss? Perhaps dumping her ageing Duke in a Queensland clinic for depression might be finally telling on her nerves.

I exchange a wink with that vixen Tat and sink back, glad that order is restored with the decanter.

'What *is* a Bogan? What does it mean—bogus? Bogie?'

'Can't begin to guess.' Tat shrugs her bony little shoulders. 'Not a Bougainvillea for sure!'

In the cheery Morning Room, affording full view of the hothouses, lawns with deer tip-toeing to fountains watered straight from the Derwent, I note the Art connoisseur Roald Lyttleton is finally here, and already pecking at his grilled kidneys. A Ralph Lauren polo matches his apricot socks and I get the impression his travelling toothbrush must have a silken tassel. Lyttleton's coif is a work of art. The silly show-off missed our last night's fun and wound up getting a taxi from Matlock station. His neatly pressed girlfriend keeps to his colour scheme so her jumper and suede booties are just a paler shade of apricot: reminds me of Harvey Nicks mannequins waiting to have their heads screwed on. Dear oh dear, no, we have no bananas. The moll collects her boyfriend's toast from the side board and says good morning to me as if relaying a weather forecast.

'There you go, Rolo,'

'Doesn't Rolo need it cutting into soldiers?' I retaliate under my breath.

The Duchess with Quentin, their backs to the breakfast table, are twittering evil insults. I know by their expressions. Sticking my nose into the pink paper, I tweak my ears at their murmurs…. Roald Lyttleton is at Cholmondeley Hall for more than a spot of Peak District air. After Quentin departs to sling lead at some sad-looking pheasants with Peter the landscapist in tow, James wobbles downstairs to join us at last.

James confides he no longer partakes in Hunting or Shooting, even though it produces a lucrative industry; he was forced to shoot little birdies as a sensitive nine-year old and it put him right off killing.

So while those goons flex their gun arms, he takes me-myself-I, Roald and Miss Shadow, on a tour of the secret parts of this palatial place where Old Masters grow fat and gilt laden. As we exit the sumptuous Jude Library, ahead of a troupe following a matron sporting an 'Official Guide' badge I hear murmurings twixt Roald and the Viscount. Sounds like Jamie Bradwick is contemplating flogging a Jean-Honore Fragonard out of sight of his Pater, the 96-year-old Earl (with a little help from his Art Critic friend?)

It is common knowledge there is little love lost between the Old Boy and his Heir. Bradwick apparently needs 'to act swiftly.' Astonishing how these blue-veined sods enjoy cleaning each other out. While the likes of little *moi* get frowned on for making an honest buck out of some petty Arts & Crafts, for goodness's sake?

I'm itching to update the QC about the deal being hatched on the priceless Fragonard. However, I can't manage to part Quentin and that lizard, Peter, from the killing fields. Perhaps they have found distractions elsewhere? There is much to amuse culture vultures in this eighteenth-century beauty alongside a prize Art Collection.

After the girly Guides call it a wrap, and pack up the stately home with its battery of alarms a white-faced Viscount Bradwick enters the drawing room in which we are gathered, two playing Mah-jong, the rest warming by the flames.

The Viscount's stammer has got the better of him. He can hardly speak. What could be so wrong? We stare like school children waiting to be told our punishment. Jamie steels himself to announce that a robbery has taken place in the public side of the house. His breathing is laboured.

He is quite shaken. He warns that the police have been summoned! We will surely be suspects - as houseguests. The reason being; the item missing is from a library unavailable to the general public! He asks politely, if we won't mind to be interviewed by the officer?

A few jaws drop. The Duchess makes a noise like a Shitzsu sneezing, I say 'bless you' like an idiot.

'Some arsy bastards bin cunning as a shit bone rat while we wh'aout chasing feathers in the woodpile, I recko?'

Fresh faced Quentin enters wearing a cravat of dizzying hues, unaware of what has transpired. Has the prat stooped to borrowing the lizard's garish wardrobe? Already!

Roald Lyttleton scoots to Jamie's side from God knows where. Ma-jong and Miss Jong forgotten. He is calmness personified.

'Well of course nobody will mind being frisked, old boy, it's the least we can do... You'll need a glass of whisky. I think we all need one?

There is something far too chummy about his manner.

'What did they *take*?'

In this veritable palace of Art, it is fascinating to know what exactly a common thief would choose? But perhaps Common is not the thief to chase?

Viscount Bradwick is on the brink of tears. I can't feel sorry. There he was slyly planning a plunder of his own property and gets pipped to the post by a far niftier thief that has time for cumbersome paintings in gilt frames.

As he tries to expand, a stutter bursts. 'I-I-I'm pr-p-p-pretty sure it was a-a-a f-f-f-First Edition of-of-ah...'

'Whaaat?'

'Yar…it's a Ma-ma-ma-Marquis de Sade…a rare edition-'

'Huh? Haw cud that be valuable? I thought yer meant a serious thievery - what's the John Dory? Spit it aout!'

'Indeed. In in-in-indeed…. This was um-um, a most valuable First Edition, Widdy…'

'Haw the heck? The place was teaming with you's Guides and hard Yakka's—'

'Quite! You see, ev-ev-every copy of-of-of every copy of *Le Philosophie Dans le Boudoir* was b-b-burnt in Paris by the p-p-p-po-po police when de Sade was put into prison. So-so it is, well it *was* the only copy. Yes, the only sur-surviving copy by Marquis de Sade!'

'A bushwhacker or what? Getting Sheepy when you's invited to a grand jobbo like Cholmon…'

'Yes, that's correct' booms Quentin, the well-read idiot. 'It was indeed the very last publication—to escape that diabolical public burning of Sade's entire collection!'

Imagine him blatantly giving that away? You'd think a man in his position would keep his trap shut.

Her Grace slaps her thigh, lifting her wide bottom off her chair just enough to release a high-pitched squeak of excess wind, with the ease of a polished thespian.

'Cat outta the friggin bag' Widdy snorts. Streuth! I s'pose you won't want this bunch of crow eaters back for a barbie anytime soon m'boy? A right Royal Flush we must seem…'

'Speak for yourself, Widdy,' I stare directly at her.

The Viscount gulps from the glass Roald has placed in his hand to stop it shaking and gazes tearfully at us, no words come... even in a stutter.

There is stony silence in which nobody can think of a thing to say to him.

I, alas, am suspect Numero Uno on account of knowing where to flog things ancient. The Duchess of Stratton and Cheatham might be unscrupulous enough to have done the deed. Quentin's daft outburst makes him appear slippery. Peter Rankin is always on the brink of some minor bankruptcy. Tat Evans may be the only houseguest to escape with a flutter of her caterpillars. Then there's Roald, Art Critic who should spot a First Edition at ten paces? If the creep was abetting Viscount Bradwick with a lucrative stunt when this precious copy of *Le Philosophie Dans Le Boudoir* was snatched he's not likely to admit it - even for an alibi.

It is going to be a long evening.

The cops will get their job satisfaction for sure. No Port to left or right tonight!
 How terribly sad to end a weekend with funny-beans like these on a nebulous note.

For the Heir of the Earl of Warwick, I guess - you win some, you lose some.

As Quintin surmised after we were eventually released by the cops and safe in his vintage chariot heading homewards,

'The boys of the Art World have the morals of il Mafiosi'

The toad stayed schtum regarding the scruples of sons of Earls and their girls.

But before you all scoot – let me say… when you're next around the Portobello Road, do drop in and say hello, won't you? It will take the tedium off an ordinary day…besides, you know me now!

You only have to look for my sign FAST & LUCE.

TO SEE THE SEA

'So what do I call you these days, Sudu Nona? Or Rosa?'

'What you always calling me Missy… I not minding when it is you. Any name I like from you….'

'What did they name you when you were born?'

'Aney, hard to know. One cousin-brother saying my name given by Hamiduru in temple is dipperent one; not remember now. Then before I three or four year, women in village calling Sudu Nona (white lady). My mother liking they call me Sudu. She also saying I light-skin from all her so-many-children's. That how I getting this name.'

'Rosa is not your birth name?'

'Rosa name - Teacher Lady calling when I working her home. Nice name Rosa—same like Western name, nether?'

'It's a flower from Engalanthe. Rose. That sweet-smelling flower growing near Nawalapitya way, have you seen? With thorns…' I mime a pricked finger.

Sudu Nona shakes her head in wonderment, her eyes sharp. Her eyes have a startling blue ring around the iris. The idea of a sweet-scented rose, however foreign, and despite thorns, appeals.

Teacher Lady is Sudu Nona's name for a village school teacher who adopted her, aged seven, after her parents died. She can't remember much of them and thinks they might simply have been too poor to bring her up. Her paler skin made Sudu an attractive proposition to be farmed out. Teacher Lady took care of her; the seven-year-old was made a servant to look after the teacher's two children until she grew up.

Sudu Nona has not been to school. Her sleek grey hair is smoothed away from her handsome face into a loose konde behind her neck. To passersby on the road five kilometres from the new cricket stadium, she radiates vitality and cheer. The flimsy, cadjan booth she has taken for her three-hour stint to sell cups of herbal *Kande* is just enough space to shelter from a gust of rain. Her heavy enamel pan sits on three solid stones, raised over a token twig fire that burns to keep the herb and red rice conjee warm. She hugs the pot possessively like it is a child. It has taken hours of foraging for Mukunuvenna leaves, its main ingredient. Sudu Nona explains that *Kande* is the first food babies get weaned on in the villages after mother's milk: now that ayurvedic cures and tonics are becoming popular with people who ride in big cars, village grandmothers sell pots of it in the early breakfast hours when workers are travelling to their factories.

Tomorrow she will make *Gottu-kolla kande*, which is the most popular.

The village mudalali who charges rent on these paper-thin shacks, is currently on pilgrimage at Kataragamma Festival to stick metal forks through his tongue and pay penance for his sins accrued for the rest of the year. Someone alerted Sudu Nona that if she brings her pan in his absence, she may get away rent free. I have come to help her set it up. Sudu Nona cannot read the cardboard sign made for her by grandchildren saying *'kande'* in curly Sinhala script.

'Bohoma hondai, ah?' I say appreciatively, giving a thumbs up. 'You could charge more for a cup than 25 rupees?'

'Grand-daughter saying same. Her teacher tell to bring and come near is-school gate-tua! But cannot go Missy, mage cacula honda nay, ne? How I carry that long way?' She rubs her arthritic legs. 'That teacher liking *kande* because make her better when she bad, bad sick'

When Sudu Nona's employer's children grew up Teacher Lady gave Sudu in marriage to a 58-year-old man. Although Sudu Nona was twenty, she could tell he was a drinking man. She worked to save enough money and eventually got away from him to marry a chair-caner with whom she had three children. Her husband is now too ill to go to work. Sudu Nona is the sole bread winner as a daily domestic in a country household. There are other domestics kept, so her work load is far reduced; and she will get a small pension when she retires. Meanwhile she feels fortunate to be allowed time off to sell her herbal *kande* by the roadside a few times a week.

'No retire me. Work up to day I die. That all I pray for!' She smiles, showing her strong, perfectly even teeth stained from years of chewing *bullath*.

Two cars travelling in tandem slow down and stare with curiosity at the floppy handmade sign. They pull up on the verge and one driver gets out. City slickers in expensive leather sandals and shorts. He produces paper cups, ridged with holding tabs for handles. The man glances suspiciously at me. I back off while Sudu Nona uses her coconut shell ladle to pour out five generous cups.

The man takes a gulp of the brew. His expression shows he isn't used to it. However, he leaves a tip. It is still far less than what he will be charged further on when he stops at Cadjugamma—where younger, dolled-up girls wearing lipstick sell Cashew nuts beside the road.

Our business woman is beaming as she waves her customers off.

'See what I mean? You can definitely charge them more, nether?'

Sudu Nona shrugs, 'Kamak nay, Missy.' It won't matter.

She explains how she forages for herbs on her employer's estate or by the wilderness near the stream. The costs of making the brew are the raw red rice and coconut milk – the nuts she will grate fresh and squeeze. Her sister used to grow the garlic and let her have it free. Last year when a bad disease came from China, the women taking cleaning jobs in seaside hotels got ill and were not allowed home to recover. Nor were they sent to the government hospital in the town. So, sister Padma, a strong worker with five grandsons, left this life at fifty-nine, says Sudo Nona, pressing her fingers against her eyelids and going silent.

'Now I oldest in family.' She sighs.

'Yes, an important position,' I say, fiddling around for a way to ask her what her age is. 'When will you be the age your sister was?'

'Me? We not haue certi-pi-cat that time. But Teacher Lady saying I sisty-year.'

'You are sixty Sudu Nona? Sure?' I hold up six fingers to verify.

Even with her beautiful face and dazzling eyes I had expected her to be a well-preserved 75-year- old. Sudo Nona has no vanity. She would not claim to be anything other than the age she is. Then she clutches my elbow and tearfully tells me about the promise her sister made before she fell suddenly ill.

Though Sudu Nona was born twenty miles from the coast, she has never seen the sea. When Padma got the chance to work at the hotel on the beach, she promised Sudu Nona she would arrange to show her the Indian Ocean the next time she left for her nine-weeks-on, two-weeks-off shift.

Sudu Nona mutters in a sob, 'Sisty years, suuure!' she strokes my cheek with her papery finger and asks, 'How much you?'

Sudo Nona scrapes the last from the pot into two remaining paper cups.

'*Kande* okkoma fin-eesh!' she announces satisfied, folding the day's takings in a secret loop of her redde she drapes around her waist.

'Cheers!' I say, lifting my cup to toast her business venture.

'Cheer-cheer! Mage Missy—you make good luck por me.' She quips so fast, for a split second I'm back in a West-country pub, draining the dregs of a more potent brew.

BEHIND THE SCENES

The Guide opened the adjoining door between our private apartments and the Main House just wide enough to let a gentleman in brogues slip in. He clutches a worn teddy-bear dressed in his own faded linen blazer.

'Mr Benjamin likes to see His Lordship' the Guide says, retreating hastily to where tourists queue to enter the main house. The heavy oak door clicks shut.

I am left to do god knows what, with this smiling stranger. He takes my hand warmly.

'How d'you do? I'm John, an old friend of this great family. I hope you won't mind me intruding?'

I reply uncertainly, 'Oh, Hello? He shouldn't be long. He's in a meeting with the estate manager…' I motion to the closed study door 'Why don't you come into the drawing room?'

'Archibald Ormsby-Gore,' the man adds, as we paced gently round the large billiard table, an island of green in the middle of the flag-stoned hall.

He does look like an Archibald. His head not quite bald but getting that way. I like his melodious voice.

'I've had a glorious morning in the Old Library. I seem to uncover something new each time I'm here. Do you frequent it?'

'If that's the one on the top floor—only when I take people to scare them for the ghost walk,' I giggle stupidly. 'I don't know my way around this place yet. It's… quite terrifying. So many stairways.'

He chuckles. 'It was built to confuse, I'm sure of it!'

I'd better ask if he might like coffee. His face is cosy, not unlike the bear.

'Well Archi—what will it be for you? A G&T or a cup of tea?' he mutters to himself.

As if by magic the Butler slips in with two pottery mugs on a tray. He may have been heading for the study, but we reach out so he stops obligingly.

'Of course, Mr Benjamin.'

So now I knew he's not Archibald. The gent is Benjamin; the Ted is Archi Ormsby-Gore. How like the English to be so ridiculous, yet I am amused by the peculiar man who seems as if he's stepped in from another century.

'Nicholas's mother and I used to be neighbours in the early days, t'other side of the Tamar… we both have Cornish roots, you see.'

'Ah, Romaine? Yes, she's a lot of fun. I have met her… er once.' We pause in front of the tarnished dinner gong and glance back at the vivid green island of billiard.

He scowls at the ludicrously large gong, Verdigris with age.

'This cumbersome thing? Not meant to be a dinner gong. It was for summoning monks from their day's travail in the fields…' His actorly voice echoes in the high-ceilinged hall.

'Really? How d'you know… did this place used to be a monastery then?'

'A Priory, it seems, in its previous life' His theatrical tones bring Nicholas out of his study.

'That's fine. I'll leave it with you-' He calls over his shoulder, extricating himself to get to us. He beams at his guest, though surprised to see him. Greeting him warmly he asks if he will stay for lunch.

'That's awfully good of you my boy, but I'm being chaperoned to London in half an hour. We won't reduce Mr Ormbsy-Gore to public transport now he's acquired such a reputation.' He winks at Ted.

Nicholas chuckles in the friendly voice he usually keeps for me.

'Well, it's a really lovely treat to see you both! I wish you would stay longer.'

Benjamin asks how the painting is going.

He clearly knows how to press the ecstasy button on Nicholas. Now they could jabber on until the cows come home, while I'm left holding a mug of coffee I didn't want. The pony-tailed host walks his guest through the blue corridor where the newest batch of murals wait to be forced into submission; sacks of sawdust and litre tins of Raw Sienna to be mulched together. Nicholas didn't see any point in spending on 'expensive colours' to create just the bases. The jewel colours which are costlier he uses like icing on top of his mud pies. Naples Yellow. Monestial Blue. Windsor Violet. Crimson Alizarin. Rose Madder: sounding so delicious I could lick them from the tube.

The sunlight from the high windows of the corridor are lighting up dust particles, dancing away from the rolled back carpet. It would start me sneezing if I followed them.

As soon as our visitor and his teddy with a nose like a Polar bear departs, Nicholas bounds back to locate me in high excitement. Such high spirits that I expect he would grab my bum under the short skirt and suggest we steal a few minutes in our secret spot on the led-lined roof we often escape to for privacy.

Instead, he asks 'And do you know who *that* was?' He can hardly contain himself.

'Yes he was collecting a bear from the Teddy exhibition up—'

'—as it happens, he was at the same Oxford College I went to!' Nicholas retorts, more like a kid with a new pair of blades than a thirty-three-year-old heir of this great pile.

'Really? Lucky old him! But hold on— Benjamin must be much older than you, right?'

'What…. did you say—Oh my god? Noooooh…' His voice is a high-pitched yelp of pain.

'You surely didn't! Oh god! You-you-you called him *Benjamin*—to his face?' His expression, which mirrors the Moncrieff ancestral portraits in the house, crumples like the saw dust blocks for his mud pies soon will do in his hands.

'Err, don't know? He should be glad I didn't call him Archibald…'

Nicholas takes my chin between his fingers, exasperated, then mouths his words in slow motion.

'It's BET-JE-MAN! The Poet Laureate John Betjeman' he snarls.

The Right Honourable Viscount is not smiling. I knew then I have got something wrong. I didn't dare imagine what it was?

'Alright, alright—Bet-je-man!' I mimic timidly 'I'm dying of hunger, Nicholas. Please can we ask if lunch is ready?'

The psychic butler rumbles the gong not intended as a dinner-gong, in the erstwhile-Priory, now half-home, half-museum. Generations of his blue-blooded family have called it home. I have slept easier in an empty railway carriage.

The Verdigris gong echoes the grumble in my stomach.

I wish I had dared to snatch a lift with that curious man and his lovely Ted in the crumpled linen jacket.

DANCING WITH THE HOLY GHOST

The cake plate at Green Cabin is not a patch on the Pagoda Tea Rooms. Yet I'm cramming in my second eclair when Daddy asks if I'm excited to be a flower girl for Ryce and Chop's big day?

I almost choke – it's that much of a surprise my brother, Ryce has found someone to marry.

'Uh? Oh, they call them bridesmaids nowadays Daddy—even when they're chooty girls of four and five.'

'I see?'

'I bet I don't get to choose my dress...'

Da hates wearing ties more than the devil himself. I tease

'Will you put on your tie?'

'En-oh! Stopped wearing them long ago. Won't matter a jot since I'm not the dad to give the…'

'Why?'

'… give away the bride. It's *the girl's* father who gets that honour'

'- okay to leave this?'

'That poor sod pays for the whole shindig' he guffaws 'Alrighty Mischief if you can't polish it off, we better scoot'

I'm relieved he seems in lighter mood for this wedding than when my sister, Flo, got married! I am longing to stand on Daddy's best shoes and dance round the room.

Yes, Mamma did make a frock without asking what colour or anything. It's too short to wear with the can-can underskirt I inherited from Aprille. There's no time for alterations so I end up in a shot-taffeta frock with tight puff sleeves. My hair is so short from the last head-lice scare that I look 'Hideous-kinky' - my cousin, Aprille's new word since she returned from London. She hasn't said what it means.

We pile into Uncle Gerald's battered mint-green Hillman and when we reach the pink church there's a hurry-scurry to line up the bride's attendants; four girls wearing matching dresses in primrose are lined up. They stand obediently behind Chops in her cream frock with a sweetheart neckline and long veil. My breakfast lurches in my chest and I'm going to be sick. Organ music bellows. Everyone stands. My throat is smarting with the acid taste and tears well up, but a voice in my head—maybe Flo's voice—is saying *you are not going to make a scene!*

I wish she was here to hold my hand. Why is my sister blighter so late?

The bride holds the trembling arm of a distinguished man. Mamma whispers 'This is Mr White….'

Mavis looking entirely different in her wedding best, mutters,

'So why the relatives didn't get a chance to meet beforehand? Mmmn… like an older James Cagney, ah?

'No dear, Cagney was short! Dan Durea, don't you mean?'

The altar boys in frilly lace smocks are waving silver incense lanterns, responding in Latin. It's like watching something on stage. I stare, as gobsmacked as I was when the school took us to see Yeoman of the Guard at Lionel Wendt Theatre. I love how the boys chant like baby angels. My crushing disappointment I have to keep to myself. At least nobody has recognised me in my moron haircut. Mamma also looks peculiar - with an eye veil attached over a smart pillbox hat, dead flies sprinkled over the net veil. Like a witch in a horror film …urg, with maroon lips.

We sit, we kneel, we sit, then all stand up as if something important is happening.
Chops turns from Father, takes her bouquet of arum lilies back from the oldest bridesmaid, links her arm with her Bridegroom and they start slowly down the aisle. Whaaat - it's over already? That's it?

Ryce grins like a bandleader in his borrowed white Tux, his teeth whiter than Mr White's hair. Why has he got that ridiculous strip of moustache? Oh yes, he's Little Richard today. I prefer him when he looks like his other hero—Evil Knievel. Uncle Bertram is snapping with a flash camera, the bulb pops. I was told that Chops had no small sisters so who *are* these girls? I wonder what stopped her choosing me?

Mamma must have told her I looked like an oily crow? These girls are so pretty in long yellow frocks - made by a better dressmaker than my mother.

While the congregation surround the couple at the entrance, I'm idling in a corner embarrassed to be spotted in this *stupidagio* frock. Ryce darts inside, grabs me by the wrist.

'Come Bubs, we have deeds to do!' he whisks me through a side door into a car with its motor running 'Have to pick up the Volks from Daddy, fast-fast.'

I'm corralled between Ryce's legs while his Usher, dressed like a cinema ice-cream seller, screeches through the back lanes. Ryce and I tumble out at the place Da has been house-sitting.

Oh no! Da is still in a dirty vest and clogs, leaning over the bonnet of his new Volkswagen. He wipes his hand on a rag and explains what he has fixed, grabbing a towel to dry his face. The bridegroom gives the spotless passenger seat a careful wipe with a duster. He starts the engine and relief spreads over his face.

I give Da a hug. He squeezes my shoulders and makes a token attempt at ruffling my hair.

'Clever Da! But you're not coming to the party like that?'

'Like what?' He's playing the fool.

'You going to dance with me - remember?'

'Ask your mother, she'll dance the jig...'

'Da, I want to stand on your shoes and dance around the room?'

'Now girlie - I have my big race to watch. Earl Grey is tipped to win. Can't miss it for all the devils in Doha!'

'Wha–at? Daddeeee... come after the race then? I'll keep a piece of cake for ya,' I yell from the back seat of the Volks Beetle which smells like a new suitcase.

Ryce drives like a bat out of hell.

Only when we reach the church with a cluster of passersby loitering to ogle the white wedding, does it dawn: without his car, poor Da can't get anywhere! Not to the reception at Mr White's home in the middle of nowhere.

The guests clustered around the bride turn to cheer at Ryce returning. A lanky boy with a flower in his buttonhole is snapping away. Ken, our cricketer cousin says 'hold it, the vanishing Bridegroom has managed to get into one final snap, folks!' calling Ryce over for the photo. Everyone is throwing confetti in the shape of anchors at the couple.

Ryce is shaking hands with the priest in a purple cassock, thanking him. The sea breeze lifting the cassock makes Father look like he's stolen my can-can petticoat.

I'm feeling cheered enough to join in the fun and get into the snap but Ryce has left the car running so I can't desert it. A teenager pops up at my window and sprays shaving foam in a heart shape. It expands to cover the window so I'm suddenly invisible! Two bridesmaids and Aprille escort Chops into the front seat. Aprille looks as dishy as a magazine cover girl, her hair in a French pleat. Ryce comes around to arrange Chops' long veil so it is pouring over her seat onto my knobbly knees in a stream of white froth. I stretch it over myself and nestle into the net getting more invisible. Aprille is laughing and pointing to me… I catch Mamma's face finally spotting me in the Volks, surprised. I wave, happy to be out of her reach. She mouths something.

Someone is calling 'Don't head for the main road. Take the *old* Panadura road!'

123

Ryce is back in his driving seat and glances adoringly at Chops, clutching her hand in ivory lace gloves,

'So Sugar-bush? You ready to beat it?' He blasts the car horn a few times. Everyone yells and throws more confetti through the open windows.

'What a gang of hooligans.... you were right!' Chops laughs.

Ryce turns around 'Oh-my-gawd, I forgot about Bubs here...'

Chops says, 'Oh, hello doll?' then, 'Crikey— wait, you made me forget my bouquet, you madman-'

'That's what bridesmaids are for. You need worry only about *me* now!'

Ryce says breezily that it's only a 35-minute drive to the clove and rubber estate. In my mind it feels like the yellow brick road while I sit still as a statue watching a dragonfly alight on the bride's veil, willing it to stay forever. After we pass the Dehiwala bottleneck, Ryce asks,

'Cat got your tongue, Kiddo?' and I don't even clock that he's talking to me till he sticks his tongue out in the driving mirror.

Chops says she's glad the hocus-pocus is behind us because she was expecting Ryce to forget the Latin response. He only recently changed faith to marry her. Chops starts trilling a song recorded by Sister Luc Gabrielle who escaped a strict French nunnery to become a pop star now known as The Singing Nun.

> *Dominique, nique, nique*
> *S'en allait tout simplement*
> *Routier, pauvre et chantant...*

How fortunate that Ryce met a nurse and one who can sing! Ever since I can remember, Ryce has been stomped by a serious motorbike accident every single year. We have got used to my policeman brother holed up in a cottage hospital or military camp ward —too remote to visit. Chops says they met when his collarbone got broken.

'Yes, I was the gentlest with injections when he was at Minneria Airfield hospital, so that's how he knew I was The One!'

When Chops laughs her voice is like a waterfall. She says Mamma approved of her even before they met owing to her reputable profession.

While we sit around the veranda pecking at June's demon Short-eats and some killer prawn balls, I'm still watching the gate for the beige Citroen to bring Biddu and my Flo. One of the guests I noticed glaring at Mamma, seemed to know Flo. She says she can understand her not wanting to be face to face with a Polygamist.

'No Aunty, that's not what she does. Flo's a Stenographer at British Oxygen!'

'Aaah? Is that so…er, and whose child are you, dear?'

'She went to the Polytechnic though. Flying colours! She's my sister - I should know!'

I find myself smiling for the first time today. My arrival with the bridal couple has raised a few eyebrows so guests seem to watch me curiously. I feel like I'm almost famous.

After we have gorged on home-made chicken Lamprais baked in a plantain leaf, Mamma and aunty Mavis start tweaking the cake which survived a bumpy ride from the cake lady. Two boys sidle past.

'How can you be sure?' one of them stares at me like I'm a dried sprat.

'Ask anyone,' his friend replies 'She's his *half-sister*'

They are not from our side of the family. The biggest secret is the one I alone share: the honeymoon couple are driving to a game reserve on the eastern part of the island beside an old elephant watering hole. Even the Best Man won't know its location in case the hooligans pitch up to surprise them. Ryce's Godfather— Emil Savundra (Uncle Mickey to us) who is currently on trial at the Old Bailey — gifted my brother his jungle shooting lodge. Ryce made Chops a promise not to touch a gun on this occasion. Instead, he's taking a batch of baby hawks in the boot, to train them to land on the head of a water monitor lizard, then hold it in its beak until it flays itself on the rocks and expires. It leaves no gunshot wounds so the lime green, silver-streaked purple skin remains flawless; for a very special pair of shoes for his sweetheart!

On their return they will spend a night at a Rest House opposite the island's highest waterfall. Chops told me later she was clutching her rosary every time Ryce unhooded the three-week-old hawk chicks. Until they are under control of their handler, they won't wait for prey. Yes, when they are hungry they can peck your eyes out.

When I smell Temple blossom which women pick to
take to temple for *puja* it reminds me of that precious
ride so close behind Chops in Da's spotless Volks
Beetle, when nobody was sure what had become of me.
It made up for not having a wreath of violets in my hair
or a bridesmaid's frock. Though I'm sad my Da
couldn't come to dance me round the room, sitting
close to the singing bride and that unforgettable scent of
Frangipani makes me feel I've danced with the Holy
Ghost.

HUGO AND HILDA

The house on the hill was beckoning to my mother.
Like you feel the rain approach. Like the monsoon
gathers. The more the villagers warned us, the more Ma
was obsessed.

     None of the boarding houses were safe for
single women in this transient town of Malays, Muslim
merchants, Bhaiya moneylenders strutting the lakeside,
stroking seven-inch mustachios and looking fiercer than
our policemen. They wore black boots with tucked
khaki Afghan pyjama-trousers: the boots terrified me.
The place we called home was one room in a cement-
floored house without proper curtains, opposite a bus
shelter. The husband worked out of town in the week
and scolded his wife for allowing us to stay.

     When he returned from the Toddy tavern to give
her a hiding he yelled 'Get those hard-up Eurasian
bitches from under my roof, woman!'

     That's why we had to go and live in the back of
beyond.

This new landlady wore a Kandyan sari. Ma said she was 'utterly respectable.' So much so, she nearly turned us down. Ma had to plead we were good, quiet folk. Since moving to this new boarding house which my sister, Kamila, renamed Casa Ludicrous, Ma devised an evening walk so I, the only child at Casa Ludo, was out of the way when the other lodgers returned. We dropped off the week-old copy of the English Times for the spinster ladies by the culvert. On days they have made Guava jelly we might get lucky staying for a cup of tea to sample the wine-coloured preserve on nicely buttered bread. At Casa Ludo we had something Kamila calls Marg.

While returning we took our time to dawdle at the river and watched the working elephants brought to bathe after their hard day's logging. After passing beneath the Mara trees which the fruit bats used for their boarding house causing an acrid stink, Ma showed sudden daring. She proceeded beyond that taboo gate the villagers avoid like a gateway to hell. Kamila and I followed, finding ourselves in a bare compound facing a cadjan hut, a mongrel dog tied outside with children playing naked in the dust. The oldest spied us and ran inside yelling, 'Amma!'

It brought a man to the doorway, startled. He spat crimson betel nut juice on the ground and glared. I didn't know what my mother said in her few words of Tamil. The man spat again, this time more in annoyance, then he bolted through a tunnel of shrubbery which led up the darkening hillside. Now the sun had gone, the light was disappearing fast. Crickets were starting their evening chorus, far noisier than at Casa Ludo.

I was glad Kamila was reticent to go inside the place, even though she had not been present to hear the village busybody.

'Ayoh, that Col-onel having a rum reputation, no? His workers running off because the children apparently have now contracted it…even ow-ur Padre stopped visiting those suddi!'

Ma frowned at the dark hole the man had vanished into. The planter's house loomed above, its shutters stared flatly over the trees like a sad, forgotten doll's house. Kamila, edging towards the gate rubbing her arms against the chill, was making my mother look uncertain.

'Maybe you are right? Not the done-thing to call so near to dinner? Let's come back during the day.' She turned.

The thud of bare feet swivelled us back. Only the man's white teeth and sarong were visible as he spoke above the roar of crickets. Ma shot Kamila an anxious look and gripped my hand. Next thing I was dragged up concrete steps, leaving the dim glow of the kerosene lamp from the hut. Kamila strode ahead to keep up with the man's swift pace. Overgrown shrubs smacked us with their fat, shiny leaves as his ascent catapulted branches at our faces. The steps twisted up the hill then levelled as we passed under a bower of ragged roses, their furious scent swamping my nostrils. It contrasted with the astringent scent from the orchard. Ma grasped my wrist too tight and cleared her throat. We fumbled around a corner, then a sprawling unlit house emerged, neglected and empty. Ma straightened and glared for signs of life on the open veranda. There were no lamps lit. Just the dark outline of a grand bungalow crusted over with vines.

We turned towards the only patch of remaining light. In a bald clearing to the side of the house, a scraggy figure, shrouded in clothes too large for her frail frame, was standing. She dangled above the unkempt lawn like a bunch of dried twigs. Still, as if posing for a photograph, she was staring blindly. Ma and Kamila stopped in their tracks. A petite servant woman was trying to prevent her patient from toppling. Neither had seen us. The scarecrow-like creature aimed her body to take a step, white gloved hands emptily resting on two sticks. When she lifted a leg, it swung loosely back and forth at the knee before finding a footing: a puppet whose strings had gone lax.

I wanted to run away but the man had reached her and muttered. Halting her dancing body, the figure turned her head stiffly, round black glasses aiming roughly in our direction.

'Miss Fraz - ahem?' Ma tried to call but her voice got stuck. She cleared her throat more to announce her presence. 'Ah, Miss Frazer? I am… Jilly Hettiarachchi. We're … friends of the Kaul's. They told us… that - that you don't go out much … might like a visit?'

The mother of scarecrows made a sound in her throat. It could have been 'Huh!'

Ma waited. When no reply came, she took another breath to soldier on in a voice so sing-along you would not dream she was wrenching my arm from its socket.

'My daughters and I take our evening walk past here, so I thought… well they said you didn't get out much so… we came to… to introduce ourselves-'

The words of the village tattlers were in my ears: 'Oh no, they wouldn't walk anywhere. They had horses sent from abroad. Now see how they're left to rot on that hill.'

No word from the curious figure. She resumed her battle—supported by the Amah—to force her limbs into a grotesque lollop to cover the short distance.

'You've lived here many years, I take it?' Ma was inching closer.

A hard, shrill sound ripped the air. I looked at the sky thinking it was a strange bird.

'No. Need. For visitors…' the puppet-lady spat. 'No one. Need. Visit. Not a thing. Anyone. Can. Do…'

The high-pitched words came from a hole in a face that appeared to be wrapped in white tissue paper. Yet it sounded like it was echoing from the empty veranda. It sent a shudder through my small body. I was pressing my legs together, urgently wanting to wee. Ma drew a sharp breath. I don't know what my fearless mother expected. She cleared her throat, then stalled, when Kamila found her voice.

'We wondered if there was …something we might bring you?' Sis began in her precise voice. She had left school early to start a secretarial course at the Tech. Already she was practising how to be a good secretary.

'…You have only come,' continued the eerie descant '…to stare! Well, sat-is-fy your   curiosity. Then go!'

The voice from six feet under the earth made all three of us twist to locate its source. Coupled with the full glare of the ravaged face that had turned to catch Kamila's voice, it stunned my sister to shut up.

She whispered to Ma 'Let's vamoose—come!'

Ma, still bold-as-brass, stepped closer to the spectacle clasping my hand.

'You need not think that of us Miss Frazer... We came to make friends.' Ma motioned Kamila to advance closer. Reluctantly my sister crept up, shielding the sight from me. I was screwing my eyes up for small glimpses; in between I had to bury my head in the safety of Ma's skirt. I had not seen anything so frightening, but her voice was the worst. It was a hollow cackle from inside something like a radio: yet her accent was like the World Service announcer.

'We only wanted to be... neighbourly?' Ma is like a terrier with a bone. 'You see dear, we are new in this vicinity and don't know many folk ....'

This last revelation softened the lady because the harsh cackle was less piercing. Newcomers. Not yet subjected to local gossip?

'Can't say... seen. Kaul gals... many years—'

I could not catch the rest from my cave in the folds of Ma's skirt.

'They want me to convey their warm regards,' lied Ma. 'Yes, they send their respects!' While she spoke, I took a peek. Then ducked back to safety.

'Respect?' That unearthly sound reverberated. 'Fear and... loathing, I expect!' she doggedly made her body ascend the steps to the veranda. '...was a time... when respect... was the order of the day.' She sounded chilled to the bone. Shivering. 'Now. Anyone. Chancing on this place. Takes a. Look and... runs.'

I would have run if Ma was not handcuffing me. Kamila stood well back.

'We haven't come to gape.' Ma had come so close it was only the Amah between them.

'I would like to visit—perhaps bring an English newspaper? Kamila gets The Times through her office. She may even come and... read to you?'

I turned to see Kamila's horrified face signing, 'No! No!'

Ma was too busy to notice, clutching me and inching toward the echoey voice.

English newspapers? Her head under the crumpled hat twitched. 'That's decent of you...' she muttered turning her back in the effort to launch herself up three steps to the empty veranda.

No chairs, no rattan furniture, just a dusty old bench against the door on one side. Ma did not plan to watch this. She was retreating, treading on my toes in her haste.

'Perhaps we may call... to bring you the papers?'

No reply. The audience was over.

Kamila scooted backwards and was beckoning us towards the hedge, teeth clenched so they wouldn't chatter.

'We better be on our way then, dear!' Ma called as if taking leave at the Vicarage tea party.

Still no reply. The Amah turned briefly and salaamed.

I deserted Ma and dashed to Kamila. At long last Ma turned, throwing over her shoulder, 'Perhaps we might call in after church?'

'We. Shall. See.'

Her answer was an impatient but distinct challenge. She did not turn.

Kamila wrapped her cool arms around me and we hurtled through the darkness of the shrubbery. My throat was parched. It was the longest fifteen minutes of my entire six years. We virtually had to feel our way down, it had turned so dark. When we got level with the lantern near the hut door, we waited for Ma to catch up. Her face was taut, her hand clutching her chest. We bolted out of the compound.

Kamila let out an anguished moan. I've never seen my big sister look so scared. She picked me up.

'Jesu Christi!' she shivered, embracing me to her. Her heart was pounding against my chest.

Neither she nor my mother could say a word until we reached the safety of Casa Ludo, where the bell was sounding to summon lodgers to the table.

Ma snapped on her chummy smile pretending we had just tripped downstairs from our room. Kamila looked about to faint as we stood to say Grace.

Ma enjoyed the shockwaves our visit to the hill caused among the locals. Soon Kamila was being applauded for her zeal—reading to the white lady three days a week after work. Word seeped out that two women — one a mere girl—had surmounted the taboo zone to befriend the suddi. Our sub-post office lady told Ma that even priests had not dared go near the diseased household since the old man died. The planter's house was a forbidden place.

When Padre Kuruppvarachi heard of our attempt, he seemed embarrassed. The Frazer family had been leading parishioners once, yet Padre had turned his back on them.

Through a Doctor Ma knew, some enlightened medics at a teaching hospital were intrigued we'd discovered these isolated neighbours. Gradually the white people living nearby came to hear about it. And us. One or two were shocked into making contributions of cash so they didn't have to get too close.

They had not talked to Mrs Govindu, the caretaker at the Ambalama.

'He was a blaggard, that Colonel. Used to horsewhip his servants. In the end nobody worked for him. Then he was bringing Tamil workers from Batti—what a jing-bang, you can imagine…that family has been stricken by God for his ill-doings.'

Though Ma nodded at Mrs Govindu, she did not want to alarm Kamila who got off one bus stop sooner to take the day-old Times to our new friend. Superstitions against the white folk isolated them from the locals, the memories of the Colonel's misdeeds were harder to erase. Kamila's boss was impressed with the guts of this nineteen-year-old, so he allowed her use of the office telephone to make any calls on Miss Frazer's behalf. Yet we remained her only visitors. She became Ma's hobby. If we were not visiting her, we were calling to collect a semolina pudding from someone. Towels from the spinsters' wedding chests were a useful donation having been imported from Britain. Then Miss Frazer made an odd request: a pair of cotton stockings! Who wears stockings in our steamy weather, Ma wondered?

After many visits to the house on the hill, the odd-looking lady became a routine part of my day. In those first weeks after our surprise visit, when Miss Frazer was so haughty and horrid, I kept having nightmares.

I never remembered it, except I recall Ma's 'cure'—to leap out of bed and switch our wireless on: that stopped me yelling and waking the household. By morning my dreams were buried deep but I faintly recall the World Service announcers soothing tones.

Another dark mystery took the nightmare's place.

Hugo Frazer, the brother described as a dashing and charismatic figure, still apparently lived in the house. Although Miss Frazer mentioned him in passing it sounded as if he was absent, with no evidence of his occupation in the dilapidated bungalow. My dutiful sister and inquisitive Ma wondered where was he?

'Must be gone to Britain for education, no? They were always riding horses from abroad. I believe that caretaker mentions a "Mahathaya". Don't know if they mean Old Colonel or another Mahathaya…'

The Kaul sisters, giving us a cup of Diyathalawa High-Grown with a slice of tea-bread, made me sit up when the least deaf sister added her side of the story: 'Makes one shudder to think we lived so close to that skulduggery, for want of a better word. In latter stages I'm told, the illness has that effect….. It's why they get isolated in those dreadful places, don't you know? Drives them to distraction…'

'Please!' interrupted the one with the tea cosy face, bringing back a top-up to the pot 'Can we change the subject? This is hardly table-talk!'

Her sister had already let slip, 'So all they can think of is S-E-X!'

Because of the emphatic way she mouthed it—under her breath—it became the first word I learnt to spell, long before I knew what it meant.

Kamila and Ma didn't notice me taking the last fig bikky on the plate. While they discussed it on the way back to Casa Ludo, Ma reminded Sis that Jesus himself walked among lepers and laid his hands to make them well. Kamila snorted 'You can take a running jump if you want me….. laying my hands..!'

The day we brought a fruit jelly I had helped Ma make, she handed over the prized cotton stockings. Miss Frazer was impressed. Her mouth, really a flap of loose skin, opened into a ghastly grin revealing receding gums. I turned away to hear a Pol Kicha magpie fluttering in an overgrown shrub. It took my mind off the sight of our friend propped in an upright chair, her back to the bedroom door from where she was released by the Amma, her dark goggles hiding the wasted face and ragged ears. If she tilted her head right or left it was noticeable that her nose did not exist, just two dark holes.

For the first time I saw her minus that felt hat she insisted on wearing. The banter was going effortlessly. I think Ma must have got the message any talk about God was not popular here.

'Good of you to procure my eye drops. Supplies of Mercury chrome long gone.' She covered a gloved hand over her mouth.

'A night nurse at the General said these were much safer. They don't use Mercury chrome for delicate areas anymore… I teach ballroom dancing at the nurse's home so I get to know the girls -'

'Do thank her.' She used that shrill voice, which echoed like three people talking at the same time.

I didn't know how she did that. It made Ma gulp. It scared the wee-wee out of me. When we left, I always had to run in the bushes to do one before our walk home.

I couldn't follow what they were so engrossed in that day…

'…so Kamila says you were formerly an author? Did you … get anything into print?'

'There are three of my books in the library.' Her mantis-like arms waved in the direction of the inner rooms.

'Really? I'm an avid admirer of Patience Strong! Another author I simply cannot put down is Warwick Deeping.' She made name sound like an exotic bloom. I took a deep breath and funnily enough I smelled an extraordinary wild lily in the late afternoon stillness.

'Can't say I have,' Miss Frazer answered stiffly '… if you were to go through the doorway—there used to be a large bookcase facing…' She pointed her skeletal wrist disguised in beige gloves.

This request made Ma shoot up from her wooden stool, grabbing and nearly tripping me over 'Oh… er, yes?'

I could tell she didn't want to go further than this bare veranda with its cast of geckos, red centipedes and stinging Kadiya ants. I however, was curious about the inside. Kamila had wondered aloud if they might have a gramophone - like English houses she'd been into.

'Let's see, my books ought to be…. on the third from the top shelf. It may be rather dusty…'

Clinging to Ma's skirt I trailed through the doorway into a dim cavernous living room. It was so much darker inside that we needed a moment to adjust our eyes; the shutters closed on the windows cast ladders of sunlight across the floor.

The walls were lined from floor to the timber rafters; shadowy books with covers like bibles. I had never seen such a multitude of bookshelves. Ma released her tight hold on me to pick up a dusty volume, blowing on each spine as she held it to her eyes to make out the title. The years of gathered dust drifted toward the slits of light slanting across the room.

The pattern of sunlight projected onto the cool tiled floor. I was used to playing hopscotch with my pretend friend. I skipped to the end of the room. There was a door that gave on to a sunnier bit of courtyard. As I hopped on and off a triangle of sunlight, I heard a scuttling, the noise a puppy might make. I wondered if they had a pet? I thought I heard a whine and a sort of panting. I stepped through the doorway into a drafty passage that opened to a yard with brooms, brushes and firewood piled up. I had never been so far inside and was pleased with my unexpected daring. Kamila wouldn't believe I could be brave too. The scuttling was persistent. It was behind the door.

The half-door was ajar. The puppy was whining, wanting to play?

I hovered, but the breeze from the courtyard opened the door. I could see into a small room, like a servant's bedroom, but dingier with an iron bed and a pile of dirty clothes. The whining sounded close? The ground was bare cement, not like the smooth patterned floor tiles of the room with bookshelves. Ma's voice kept calling titles of books and the distant reply from the veranda went, 'No, not that one, keep going…'

I felt safely assured to keep on.

Behind the door a bundle of clothes lumped on the floor, moved… I searched to make out wet drool and a misshapen head, like a boiled egg that has cracked in the water with the white eggy blobbing out.

141

The lump of putty that was a sort of face wobbled in a sad stare. From a hole where there should be a mouth, a steady dribble of saliva fell onto a dirty pyjama shirt. It might once have been a blue stripe on white but was grubbier than any beggar in the market place.

I was transfixed, not believing I was seeing this in an English household. He tried to scramble back onto the iron bed by dragging himself on hands and knees. The hair had fallen out and left his head looking like a demented baby. Without the disguise of stockings, mittens and a hat, the wounds and sores protruded. I was rooted. My throat so dry I could not even call out. The Blancmange thing panted and wheezed and, at any moment, might burst into a thousand particles of jelly.

It had not dawned on me that this blobby, pudding creature, crawling helplessly on the floor was what remained of Hugo. I stood there petrified, gulping for air, unable to look away, until I felt my mother behind me, gasping.

Then I was dragged to the veranda.

'Maybe I should ask the servant to find you a torch?' Miss Frazer was saying from the veranda.

'Ah… yes- I think I have found your… books,' Ma gulped, griping two cloth-bound volumes. She fumbled in her handbag and brought out cologne to dab on her temples. Ma inhaled deeply.

'Er, yes… let's see. What lovely bindings?' She was trying to sound carefree. Her hands were shaking.

'Did I hear my brother out there?'

'Mmn…possibly … hope we didn't disturb him?' Ma was white knuckled, gripping the bench in an effort to steady herself. She looked like she wanted to run, but kept her voice even. A tear fell off the end of her nose.

I had my back to Miss Frazer and stood as stiff as a sentry at Ma's knee, facing the doorway.

'As I told you, he is bed-ridden…'

(What does it mean, bed-ridden? He was not on the bed? She means floor-ridden.)   That melty-face inside is…. her brother?

'That is sad, yes… so-um…' Ma searched for something to say.

'The disease gets a firmer hold if you contract it young,' she croaked softly, as if sensing my mother had seen more than she bargained for.

'I see… so your brother is the younger?' Ma lunged to sniff her vial of 4711.

I thought she was about to drink some. I switched back to that first mind-boggling meeting at dusk when we came across the planter's daughter. Ma was trying all she could to be friendly. Now our poor friend was trying to be chatty to make us feel better and Ma wanted to bolt.

'-was eighteen when father died. Soon after we noticed he was stricken. Since he lost the use of limbs a… impossible to give him exercise…'

'That is very… difficult for you, my dear…'

'Family of servants do a splendid job— considering they were never servants in the house.'

Ma frowned, trying to make sense of this.

'Remarkably loyal. Haven't been paid for years… live off whatever they can get for the fruit...'

'Urr… your family never had tea estates, then?' She stared glumly at the floor, disappointed.

'Father was a Planter. Tea Estates were near Horton Plains. Mother found it so cut away from things... Bought these fruit orchards— to retire to. Business became thriving. Supplied hotels in Colombo as well as… exporting.'

143

'My goodness—more profitable than the tea, I should think?'

'I was never involved—now it's too late. It rots—the fruit—on the trees. Mangosteen's go—only the Mangosteen's. The rest…' Her echoey cackle reverberated between us.

I saw my mother shudder. I tried to climb on her knee.

'What I don't understand—I hope you don't think me talking out of turn but—why—what makes you want to stay on? I mean, what made a family like yours—from abroad… what attracted you to… here, when the home country is so much better a place?'

Miss Frazer laughed the ventriloquist laugh, like several voices cackling at each other. It was like a cry of pain and sent a shiver through my body.

'We had ceased to have much contact with Britain. All my parent's connections were here—I've never felt at home on the occasions I was forced to go back … It seemed foreign to me, Blighty.'

'Ah? I see what you mean…' Ma didn't fool me. How could anyone forsake England? The land of rich milk in glass bottles on your doorstep! Where bus conductors say hold-tight-lovey and never cheat when they give you the change. And real snow falls on Christmas day!

'So what happens to these acres of Mangosteen's and Avocados?'

Ma can't abide waste. Specially now we are so poor we can only afford plantains for the fruit bowl.

'When father died—word got around. No one wants the fruit. They say its tainted.' That hideous laugh again. 'They actually believe if they eat the fruit from our orchard, they will be contaminated!'

Ma was silent while Miss Frazer made a sneeze or a cough which sounded like the noise of a battagoya, while holding a handkerchief to her face. 'The Periyasamy family take the fruit to the other side of the river where lorries collect from plantain growers near the mangrove. Yes, they were formerly our estate workers but the only ones… not to desert us.'

'…They'll get their prize in heav— um m…' Ma felt strong enough to stand at last. She let me sniff her hanky soaked in cologne.

 A baby mongoose darted from a bush by the rose bower in search of its mother. I pointed, but Ma didn't look, busy edging towards the steps. I gave one last inquisitive glare at the darkness of the room with bookshelves to make sure nobody was lurking. It was the first time she had spoken in so long. I didn't know whether Ma was up to hearing anymore? Her cologne bottle was empty. I looked round the floor for a spill but couldn't see one.

'Shall I hand him the jelly, so the flies don't settle, Hilda?' Ma used her name! I didn't know that she knew it.

'Can't understand our need for soft foods— never cooked for Europeans so one can't expect….'

Ma was eager to get away. The smell of my encounter with the blobby bundle hung in the back of my throat.

Miss Frazer and Ma exchanged words that made no sense.

'No, it's thanks to you!' Hilda concluded with a grisly grimace I thought she intended for a smile. Then she asked Ma to be sure to pick the Hibiscus which she knew from its scent was in bloom.

Ma was glad to be off and didn't stop for Hibiscus. I took the garden steps two at a time, and reached the bottom before her.

It was the only time I saw Hugo. The stench in that dingy room followed me home… a putrid cloying smell. It hung like a cloud wherever I went. Then other people at Casa Ludo started sniffing,

'What on earth is it, ah?'

'Ayoh… maybe a polecat has fouled under the roof tiles, no? Chee, Chee!'

'It may be Durian ripening in that kalle in that backside,' a lodger offered.

'Yers, yers! Last year also we got this rotten smell. Everywhere we were looking to see if a rat was dead in a corner or what? To find Durian trees growing wild' our landlady agreed.

'What a waste, ah?' Ma joined in to cover her embarrassment of bringing a stink-patch little girl home: I knew she was thinking of mangosteen and avocado rotting on the trees.

I exhaled hard to escape the stink. It was small comfort that others could smell it too. I didn't enjoy the looks from them, as if they thought I'd done ka-ka in my pants. Ma led the way up the iron backstairs used by servants to our room. Kamila was already home, perched on the banister. She had her mug of tea and was gazing into the juicy green of the kalle. She took minute sips from her steaming mug, but drank in the slice of emerald in greedy gulps.

'Sight for sore eyes, ah?'

I raced towards her for my hug but Kamila held me at length.

'Chee! Wait, wait—you must have trampled something? Let's look under your shoes?' her face turned sour 'What a putrid stench!'

'Durian is ripe - Rani says. That smells like dead men's feet, no?' Ma sniffed.

Even after my evening bath and a dollop of the stronger cologne which Ma used on Sundays—Blue Grass, the cloying stink could not be shifted. That night I dreamt of creatures with faces like perished fruit. Fruit nobody wants. The smell that filled my every moment, stopped as curiously as it began a few days later…

It was the morning when Periyasamy came bearing a message.

Miss Frazer's brother had passed away.

Hilda sent Kamila a note to ask if she might help make arrangements for her brother's burial. To get an undertaker to accept the job was impossible. No one wanted to be involved. No priest of any denomination would perform a funeral. Padre Kuruppvarachi refused permission to bury him in their cemetery. There was no time to waste in this heat.

Kamila, accompanied by the post-mistress's uncle, ventured across the suspension bridge at Dodangwella where the fear of the Colonel's history had not spread. It used up Kamila's entire Saturday to do this good deed for the man she had never seen. She returned with a gravedigger procured from a distant hamlet. Hilda asked to be carried in a chair to the burial spot, but Ma who stayed to comfort her persuaded our sad friend against it. She told us later, if the gravedigger caught sight of the white woman and guessed it was the *sudda,* he'd surely run away before completing his task.

Ma, Hilda and Amma recited the 23rd Psalm which Amma knew in English, before the Colonel's son was wrapped in jute sheets and laid to rest in a trench between the Eucalyptus and the Ceylon Oak. As Hilda directed.

The memory of that meeting with Hugo was enough. We said prayers at the rock grotto behind Casa Ludo. Ma and Kamila had wet eyes as they sang three verses of There is a Green Hill Far Away.

'There was no other good enough to pay the price of sin,
He only could unlock the gates of heav'n and let us in.'

CONTRABAND

I smile, hesitatingly holding my arms out. What will it be this time?

The kind person hands it over. Mammy watches with that expression to make me remember P's and Q's or this will be the last time anyone will bother giving you a prezzie, Scallywag.

I've been trained to give a commendable performance, not betraying the great disappearing trick to unfold. I grin uncertainly. Contain your excitement and don't dream of ripping that paper. If you tear the cellophane what good is it to anyone? No throwing away shop tags. Slowly does it, that's right. Helpful adult fingers aid my wrestling with the bow so I can undo it and see what it is: Thank you… it's what I've been wanting…

They say, I knew you'd want one because you are just the age. Are you six yet?

I was six when Reverend brought his two girls to my party. Their gift was a book with black drawings called *Alice in Wonderland*, too grown up for me to read.

Mammy took it to a child who can read properly. I was sad about that book because it felt special.

I wanted it.

Mammy has been in recycling mode, long before it became the thing to do.

If the gift arrived devoid of clues, her restless feet pound the pavements between the Buddhist temple and that new toy Emporium till she locates the shop, then she will harass the man to exchange goods. I learn early how to grovel. When the haggling reaches stalemate, I know it is time to raise my eyes pleadingly.

But not possible cash Nona, only goods to the value… was music in Mammy's ears as she sailed through the aisle to peruse utilitarian trifles—Zip fasteners, rick-rack braid, Petersham ribbon or if nothing appeals, yards of lining stuff is always handy. When she isn't tempted, some 'decent' handkerchiefs suffice. I was never shown the indecent variety.

Transaction completed Mammy's humour was improved enough to splash out on a rickshaw ride for our joyless journey back. She did this after the dentist extracted my tooth, saying ice cream will make the pain go away. Mammy could not afford both a visit to the ice cream parlour and a rickshaw ride back. I didn't get the ice cream that time. The sweating, exhausted rickshaw runner whose legs look thinner than a kitchen ladle had to jog in bare feet on the melting tar road. The younger ones - who don't usually travel as fast as older experienced men, wrap pieces of bike tires around their feet, tied round with string.

I returned to my makeshift toys, the friends who stay with me forever—an inner tube of an old tyre, unusual stones from the river, best of all, my shop of various coloured empty bottles that afford me hours of play as an apothecary, a hairdresser lady or a *The-butik* man. The old chap with cracked heels and a stoop who turns up on the back porch once a month was my only source.

We called him Boothele Man because the whole street knows he is on his way when his bike bell accompanies his cry of *Boothele? Boothele?* After he had exchanged the empty beer, lemonade and gin bottles for a few cents he had no use for the small, vari-coloured ones from smelly ointments and cough medicines. I spent my time filling them with sand or tiny pebbles or more to the point, if I wanted to be an apothecary, water that magically turns amber, green or brown.

Family members knew better than to proffer gifts not solicited by Mammy for fear they'd be made to return them to the shop themselves! Mammy chose Godparents who could in no way endanger her ploy. The two I was allotted left for far-away Toronto months after they had given me the silver napkin ring with my birthdate engraved. No sooner had they reached a safe distance, they would fire off packages for Christmas and Birthdays. This unexpected Manna came dotted in airmail stickers, foreign stamps and best of all— crimson sealing wax I'd snap off in sharp pieces to hoard for invented games.

The orgy of savaging the unreturnable boxes and stripping cellophane to shreds was an unexplainable delight. Yet the foreign mail tailed off when my Mammy became friends with the postmistress of Mahillapitiya sub-post office, perched on the cliff that fell steeply to the river. I never found out if she did a deal to swop my impressive parcels for a postal order.

I tapped into a fresh source of contraband when my father was allowed to visit me again. Since Da was not used to amusing a small girl, he took refuge in the gaudiest toy shop. I was allowed to plunder a million bits and pieces before our next stop: Tea at Pereira's. To get treated like a Bona Fide customer at the toy shop was new.

The face of the grinning assistant who gathered my loot into a tea chest was also unusual; the shopkeeper was suddenly Da's best pal! I was returned home over excited, over tired and put directly to bed with hardly a chance to unwrap the treasure.

When I woke, the tea-chest and its contents had vanished..... Not even the tiniest bag of marbles left.

Later in life I get invited to other children's birthday parties where they played a game. A tray brimming with small objects was shown for a few heavenly minutes. Then they were covered over with a dishcloth; you had to recall what they were. It seemed a cruel reminder of my early adventures to town with my father. Each time Da mustered the courage to visit we repeated the exercise; for that was what it amounted to now, an exercise for sharpening myself at future party games? Each night that greedy cousin of the Tooth Fairy swoops down and cleared them off.

Just once, the bad fairy slips up!

Imagine my astonishment on getting up the morning after the obligatory spree, resigned to knowing the pile under my bed had floated into thin air, then to slide my foot against the bedpost and discover underneath, the most adorable slippers with beaded Chinese embroidery! I spotted them in a shop of paraphernalia on the way back to the car, Da staggering with the now-you-see-it, now-you-don't tea chest containing the glory of the kingdom.

Da had told me he was spent out, but not completely. The moment I tried on the red satin slippers I turned into a fairy Princess and insisted on wearing them to the car.

Here they are still under my bed. No dream!

A shiver goes from the top of my head to my toes. Streetwise kids might have had the sense to hide the precious red satins in a cupboard? To only take them out when Mammy wasn't about? After breakfast, iron claws grasped my wrist to march me into town. I was made to show Mammy where those satin mules came from. She puckered her nose at the film of grit on the dainty soles to harangue the Chinese lady who speaks no English for a full refund please, due to the red slippers being 'shop soiled'.

Years later, I coveted the most absurd shoes to lay my feet on.

Although my lifestyle dictates footwear for steep, cobbled streets of our hilly town and the nearby woods that unfold from my garden, shut away in the dark of a walk-in closet live my secret friends —my *toys!*

Highest suede heels with diamanté globes. Snakeskin gladiator sandals. Kid pewter-coloured pumps. Hand-tinted loafers by Manolo. The tapestry slip-ons from Florence which Lisa bought when we reconnected years after she learned of my warped childhood. When nobody is awake, I sneak into the darkened recess of this locked closet to snatch a treasured glance and a fondle.

PRINCESS ON A SHOESTRING

I have kissed a few frogs between Margaret River and Mandalay. Not even one turned into a Prince.

In the naughty, sexy 60's when all the world was a stage, a desperate movie bitch had to fetch up at Shepperton Studios at ungodly hours. One of the frogs-in-waiting spent a ransom on a white Sprite for my seventeenth birthday. Yet without my driving licence, I could only whiz round with L plates and a bona fide driver present beside me. Even the most attentive consort was not keen for a wake-up call at four a.m.

Passing the Test proved tricky if you turned up in Biba smoky-blue suede knee boots and quaint Mary Quant hot pants. I became a serial failure. My instructor at the British School of Motoring however, was delighted with my custom. He had a nickname for me, once test number six passed us by.

No, it wasn't Oops-a-Daisy. My lack of prowess was bringing in a consistent income to that sleepy branch of BSM in Westbourne Grove.

They called me 'Princess' behind my back and applauded my ineptitude. I had failed at various Test Centres from Bristol to Wembley during my first year of instruction. When my Provisional licence lapsed, my instructor—helpful as ever—filled the form to request a fresh one. In jaunty mood that day he wrote 'Princess' beside Title, handing me the form to sign. My replacement red provisional licence arrived. I tore the buff envelope to see it was in the name of Princess Surangani. From then on when I needed to prove identity for writing cheques (bank cards were unknown) out came my Provisional licence. And down went the long red virtual carpet.

That feeling of being a Fake becomes second nature to an immigrant starting a new life. The not belonging, the fear of being found out, never leaves you completely. While I was struggling to be accepted as a British citizen it seemed less of an issue whether it had to be as Miss, Ms, Mrs or er… Princess? The diminutive red folder—no bigger than a credit card—was a magic carpet. I flew though Fenwick's with arm loads of tights and Paco Raban belts, while at that shop posh, I was treated like a right Royal. Anywhere I presented my National Westminster cheque—backed up with my Provisional license—I was greeted with increasing R-e-s-p-e-c-t. Being naive, it didn't occur to abuse it. Perhaps occasionally, to book a table in a packed restaurant? And what name please? Princess Surangani? Certainly….

After practice runs through rough patches of Shepherd's Bush and skimming past Stonehenge at weekends, the day dawned a month before my eighteenth birthday.

I had worked in an actual movie and chummed up with a young actress out of *Lamda*. I'd (squeamishly) accomplished my first screen kiss with a soon-to-be staple of British television, John Thaw, in an Arthouse film playing at The Paris Pullman *Praise Marx and Pass the Ammunition*. I'd had the role of Donald Sutherland's Haitian accomplice in a TV series starring Alexandra Bastedo. Yet my new agent advised me not to accept a role in a risqué musical to be transferred from Broadway to the West End stage called *Hair*.

It needed actors to disrobe on stage! He warned that I would not be taken seriously if I accepted a part.

I was anxious at being undone by the Highway Code.

I ditched my whizzy Sprite for this important date—my eighth Driving Test in the same year.

I didn't know the staff at BSM Westbourne Grove were running a book on the chance I might pass. An Automatic Mini was provided to give me an advantage. They explained a new law was coming into force for Tests on automatics and thoughtfully procured the last available date before the old law was overridden. One of my advisors said a mini-skirt and thigh boots might be pushing it. I turned up attired in a turquoise velveteen trouser-suit.

I nervously said hello to my examiner, Mr. Savage. He made small talk as we traipsed to the parked BSM Mini. He'd been serving out in Penang and had sailed all around the East, he told me, probably to put me at my ease?

I gritted my teeth to recall which country Penang belonged to, when Mr. Savage blurted,

'May I ask— of what country was your father the King?'

I slid the gear stick into D, checked my mirror diligently. Gave my hand signal for Right and pulled away. My throat was locked in P.

'Mmmn oh, my father? …err yes, King of Lanka.' The lie tripped off my tongue. The automatic-mini ascended the hill. 'Before Independence, of course' I muttered, sweet as sugar cane.

'Those were the days, eh? Well, my ship called in at Trincomalee. I really wanted to see the island. I had heard about Ceylon from our senior Naval crew….' Savage continued in jolly vein - no longer putting me at ease. 'I caught malaria by the time we arrived in Trinco. So I wasn't allowed off the boat! The rest of the lads came back with such stories…'

'Oh, what terrible luck!' I exhaled a grateful sigh.

'I did get a look at Jaffna, though. Bought fantastic cigars off the lovely Tamil lasses hand rolling them in the square. Saw Delft Island and the wild ponies who had been left there by the Portuguese, it seems. Took that tiny ferry at Punkudutivo. What a place, eh?'

The cigar rolling girls must have tickled the savage breast of Mr. Savage. He ticked my Hill Start off his list. The rest of my test was questions about the Kandyan Court; how many wives a Buddhist King is allowed? Were concubines' part of our culture? How I must miss my life there…

I agreed that I missed certain aspects very much.

'Such as what, in particular?' Savage asked eagerly.

Difficult to concentrate on this task while being interviewed as a phony Princess. My admittance interview to The Actor's Workshop in Ladbroke Grove was nothing as demanding.

'I kinda miss… stuff like— you know, riding my elephant, Samirakand…'

He drew in an astonished breath.

'Yes, Sami was much safer than …the rickshaws. And quite a bit higher.'

Mr Savage bellowed in good cheer.

It was now time to demonstrate my skill in reversing. I was nervous—even with an automatic gearbox at my disposal.

Savage had one pressing question. Did I have any sisters back home?

I could see where this was leading; I replied all my sisters were married ones. He switched to questions about Test Cricket pronto.

When I steered the automatic Mini back to base, Mr. Savage released a smile of pure wonder.

'I have pleasure in informing you that you've duly passed your DVLA Test!'

I shook the warm, damp hand of Mr Savage without flinching.

The following week DVLA posted my spanking new driving licence made out to Princess Surangani.

I was getting used to being a fraud. And a tad addicted to the fringe benefits of a phony status. However, I did return this treasured item when one of the frogs I smooched turned out to be a Prince among Princes. He worked like a charm on me. I wondered if I could be in love? He made requests in the gentlest voice I have ever heard. I was certainly under his spell so when he suggested I ought to decline my fake handle, I put up no fight.

Not long after sending my red cloth-covered driving licence back to DVLA we became wed and under his influence I became a right little Mrs.

159

COBRA WOMAN

When I first see Arleen's stark, white-washed chapel with no twiddly bits it reminds me of the mad lady's annexe. My mother, dressed for Sabbath Worship, is feeling self-conscious without her habitual pillar-box red lipstick. She was miffed she had to remove it but perks up when introduced to the smiley American Pastor clothed in jacket and tie.

Just as Selma jollies up, heart-of-gold-Arleen, turns po-faced. She introduces my mother as Sister Selma, calling the men Brether this, Brether that and Selma parrots her. An American accent works magic on Selma. Takes her back to when GIs were sent during the war with chocolates, stockings and cigarettes. One of the best times of her life, she's told me, since there was no war on this island while Europe was in chaos. As the congregation are finding their seats, I strain to catch Selma breaking out in *Gee Whiz! I sure do, honey! Heck, yous kiddin' me?*

Selma and her pretty sister Charmaine picked up these expressions from the fast-talking swanky Yanks, who wound up the gramophone to dance to Babyface, You Made Me Love You or Goodnight Irene! Nobody had to wake up early for missions. They were here to protect the world's third largest harbour of Trincomalee, long before I was a twinkle in my father's eye. These Brethren in this soulless white chapel are intent on celebrating Sabbath with an organ; no gramophones, no naughty dancing. Charmaine would have been disappointed for sure, no kiddin'!

While waiting on hard wooden benches for the service to begin, Aunty Arleen explains a few chosen ladies will congregate in a room at the back to wash the men's feet. This is a special occasion to celebrate Martha who loved Jesus, so she did the same thing. My mother eyes light up, maybe hoping the blue-eyed American's may exchange stockings and goodies in exchange for the ablutions.

I ask why he is called 'Pastor'. Nobody answers.

When I am let out after the Saturday-School with Arleen's younger son, Emlyn and two pasty-faced girls, chewing gum, Selma is nowhere. My nylon net frock is itching unbearably. The armholes are tight. I cannot wait to tear it off and sink into the coolness of our river behind the tea estate. Emlyn and I have our heads in our hands, fed up and sweaty on the front steps by the time the well-washed Brethren filter out. Emlyn's brother Honiton comes out grinning, glad to have escaped.

'She's already accepted!' He is wide-eyed, skinny shoulders hunched.

'Whadya mean - accepted to whaad?' I hear myself duplicate my mother's phoney accent.

Emlyn has showed me the cement baptism tank and described what happened when Honiton was initiated into their new religion. Imagine getting your best clothes soaked to be baptised? Besides, the tank is five feet deep, not safe for a non-swimmer with high heels. Selma will be livid to ruin her new outfit which cost her a new Butterick pattern.

'Gone in the back…' He signals a tiny room with a high window 'Adults only taken…'

'You mean the tay-ank?' an American voice in my throat persists.

Emlyn smirks and raises an eyebrow.

'Nooo Dimwit, that's for Baptism. She was invited to join Blessing of Martha.' He curls his mouth in a smug smile but offers no more.

Selma's eyes are like stars when saying long-winded goodbyes to the tallest Brethren who bends in two over her on the chapel steps. It never takes much to keep her happy when there's a Church or Chapel close, no matter which religion: even a Hindu kovil or a Buddhist temple is enough to put her in a mood for a chat with Her Maker. I can't be sure which she prefers; praying to Her Maker or telling everyone how much she prays. Selma likes anything that reminds her of her sins. She twists round to gaze at Brother Kevin, giving him an eyeful of her shapely legs in the highest heels of any ladies present. He flashes a hundred and fifty gnashers in reply. I whisper to Emlyn,

'So do all American people have such white teeth?'

I'm itching to know more about this foot-washing ceremony. Maybe I haven't done enough sins to qualify yet?

If it is like the footbath Selma soaks her corns in, after rubbing that cream to get the dead skin off, it will not be a polite thing to talk of. Sister Selma sashays to Arleen's station wagon parked under the only tree spared when levelling the land for this bleak chapel. She climbs in the front seat beside Chappie who is fanning himself with *The Racing News*.

Arleen sulks behind. Emlyn and Honiton are jammed into the rear of the car. Arleen signals me to lay back against her clammy bosom of pillows. Chappie steers the Vauxhall Princess away from the Katugusthota Saturday bottleneck. The seats are sticking to my thighs: the heat has brought out the smell of wet dog so even a sniff of Arleen's Lavender Fields is preferable. She murmurs words like Angel, Sweetheart, Blossom, Girlie-of-mine, while absent-mindedly kneading me like a gorilla playing with its food. The exertion of bending and washing Brethren's feet has begun her wheezing.

Arleen and Chappie's bungalow at the top of a tea estate has always been magical. I call Arleen 'aunty' because she's an old family friend. She likes having us stay. The time before this, Arleen wanted my mother to let her adopt me and I got scared when I realized that she was not joking. I've always wanted a younger brother or sister but two brothers could be fun with so many trees to climb. Soon after we arrived from the train station and I managed to get the boys to myself, they disclose the star attraction: an odd person staying in their annex. They are forbidden to speak to this Basket Case so resort to spying on her. This has us occupied for most of a week and yet, I did not see her. Each time they relate a scrap of scandal —it grows more alluring. Certainly, the adults also mock the guest Arleen calls 'The Virago'.

The moment the women retreat to the bedroom for a siesta after lunch (baked Parau fish, Jak mallung, Cardamom pillau, pumpkin curry) we escape. The Mahaweli ganga flows through a chasm where the valley is too damp for tea cultivation and waterfalls keeps it icy. Emlyn can't wait to leap into our shallow pond, beside Devil Ears – two pointed rocks. After a few shrieks to acclimatise we dunk into the smarting icy water. Emlyn is already regaling his brother with a dramatisation of the foot washing.

'Aooh, brother Kev, may the Lord bless you for bringing me comfort… and while you're about it Brother, could you give my knees a scrub? Oh higher, yes just up a bit from there!' He places two round stones on his bare chest and cocks one knee daintily over the other.

Honiton guffaws.

'There's no mistakin' me Irish boobies, Brother Honey bunch. I warmly welcome you to try these juicy boobies…'

I don't want to be reminded of how flirty my mother was with the tall Brether on the Chapel steps so I retreat to the shallows. Honiton surfaces from a dive off one of the Devil Ears and splashes water at the clown. Our highlight of the day has not turned up. The boys promised a likely day to spot Basket Case because being Sabbath, she knows the family does not come river bathing. When they've worn out their antics and still no sign of her, Honiton gathers us, switching on his big boy voice.

'Mustn't stay long. On the seventh day God rested. This means we must respect—you hear that Dimwits?'

We grunt agreement and sluggishly plod up the bank leaving the smell of wet rocks and moss. Black-headed Munias whizz back and forth in the long *illuk* grass on the bank, not afraid of us. It's their territory, so they go about their business. So do the woodpeckers. The boys have been showing me many different sorts of woodpeckers here. There is a type you hardly see because it is so titchy. It's called the Pygmy woodpecker; and there it goes again.

'You hear that, don't you?' Emlyn asks.

'That's it...' Honiton nudges me to recognise the distinctive tapping. Two days after I get here, I sit sandwiched between the boys on a high garden wall opposite Basket Case's boxy concrete annexe while they describe lurid scenes of behaviour, which they swore they had witnessed. What I wanted to see most was *her* standing up to pee like a man. That's a trick I have failed to accomplish even though I'm going to be nine in a month.

Below us the yellow river zig-zags round a pebbled cove with overhanging rocks. As we drag ourselves past a bend, I catch sight of a stout, mannish figure with tight, curly hair, hunched over a pile of wet clothes, naked to the waist. I guess by the boy's trance-like state that this is the Basket Case. Why on earth did they not tell me that she was an English person! She has her back to us and is dashing clothes against a flat rock like the *dhobies* wash sheets. I can see why it makes her intriguing. But why does this foreigner want to stay with them if Arleen can't stand her?

The boys go rigid like cardboard cut-outs of Tweedledee and Tweedledum while Basket Case is unable to hear anything but the flowing water around her.

Her neck and shoulders are more tanned than the white skin that would hide under a blouse. A pair of khaki shorts not unlike those Chappie wears for work covers her bottom half. A low strangled noise is emerging from Emlyn and I turn to see him choking with silent shrieks of laughter.

'Shut up you fool-'

I am fascinated by her every move; it's a bird's eye view so I can just see the top of her head, and it looks like she has not combed her hair for months.

'You see the spade over there?' Honiton holds tight onto my shoulder in case I lose my balance on the ledge. 'She takes it everywhere with her…'

'To dig for gems.' Emlyn nods.

The woman turns squarely to face our direction making the boys double up. Her boobs are no competition for their mother's plump chest. I am surprised that she's doing anything as mundane as washing clothes on a rock? She looks peaceful and I feel a bit guilty about spying; she only has a spade and no bucket. I remember the frustration of it when I was taken to the seaside.

Honiton is chortling into his towel in an effort to mute himself, his bony shoulders jerking. Unable to control himself he makes a grab for my neck and Emm's to steer us from the greatest show on earth.

As we scramble up the slope to the house, Selma's high voice rings out from the back veranda

'Honeee! Where are you children? Honee – ton!'

Emlyn darts behind a shrub to hide our towels so Honiton has to take the brunt of the scolding from his Pa.

'Are you crazy or what, taking this poor child out in the heat of the day? She will end up with sunstroke, men! You are looking to get a thrashing with my belt or what?' Chappie tries to sound fierce.

I climb on Arleen's lap in the Planters chair to deflect her rage.

'Little petal. Look she's perspiring like anything!' Arleen runs her onion scented fingers through the damp in my hair and dabs at me with a large flapping collar.

'Stupid boy!' Arleen's cheek bulges like she has an abscess.

'Only mad dogs and Englishmen go out at this time of day. You know perfectly well you must wait till after four o'clock!'

At the mention of 'Englishman' I imagine Chappie has rumbled us.

Selma is jumping out of her skin in anticipation for another session of toe-tickling. Heart-of-Gold-Arleen has my mother worked up about a visiting Canadian Pastor who has strange effects on his congregation—— some faint, pass out, sign away their lifesavings to the preacher. Selma irons her navy skirt with a slit up the back, three times over. She has sneakily varnished two coats of Nearly Natural Cutex on her toenails. Before this event, Arleen forces her sons into their estate wagon and escorts them for a mid-week dose of religion called 'Vespers'. A young man in safari jacket from the Tea factory has arrived to drive them. I have a picture in my mind of Brethren inside the spartan chapel astride their Vespa scooters with feet resting in plastic foot tubs. In their arms are lady's silk stockings draped over like the pavement hawker's parade their wares.

The moment the estate wagon is out of sight Chappie fishes out his Special Reserve Arrack hiding in an old ginger beer crate. His guffaw is reminiscent of his eldest son as he hands Selma a glass, with a conspirator's wink.

'Thank you, Chappie, no rocks for me. Yes, I wondered how you managed, after all these years as a hard-drinking man. My, what a sacrifice that must be!' she takes an eager gulp and licks her lips, happy to be excluded from the Vespers.

Chappie confides he is not totally convinced about the ways of The Brothers of Christ. He does not mind the boys being involved since it keeps the vagabonds out of mischief, but he's uncertain how it can benefit an old sinner like himself.

I loaf in and out at random, enchanted by the family of near transparent geckos parading the wall. Arleen would ask me to fetch the gadget she keeps for murdering them with a slap. She swears they are poisonous. A family she knows had a child die when a gecko fell into a pan and got cooked in the curry. How could they be poisonous when they look so cute?

'…you don't say—this cretin was schooled in Britain?' Selma asks, astonished.

'Nah!' Chappie blows his nose in a thing the size of a duster. 'Would have been, if only she stayed put…'

'Was she deranged or wha-?'

'Nothing of the sort! Apart from going to Blighty to find himself a wife, James Faultless spent the better part of his life out here in the tea country, starting as a "Creeper". They forgot this poor child had never even seen England except in pictures on a Christmas card!'

Perched on the arm of Selma's rattan chair, I watch the baby gecko ambling where the wall meets the rafters. He's been in the same spot for the last half an hour. I wonder if he is dead or just asleep?

'So, when did she go peculiar?'

'Not *pissu* at all, I'm telling you! She got sent to England at a hideously young age, because the brother was going. He was seven. The English are the limit - with their boarding schools and what have you. She was a lost case from the word go. Had to fetch her back after she had some breakdown and never wanted to see England again.'

When I come back to the veranda in my PJs ready for bed, Chappie is only dimly visible by the glow of his cigarette, but my mother has now joined him in his smoke.

'It's hard to imagine, isn't it?' Selma is holding her cigarette high in the air pretending she's a film star, her thoughts millions of miles away '- that this same creature who prances about half-naked like a bloomin' *veddha* had a decent life and proper parentage?'

'It was completely Pukka, I can assure you. They had a grand life here…. the big planters house with minions and whatnot…'

'How does someone sink so low, I ask you?' she shivers and grabs me to sit on her knee, pressing her fingers against my sore, throbbing throat. 'So that is all the home she's got? - in Angoda…'

'Yers, yers, now her family have cast her out. Because of her white skin they allow her to share a small bungalow on the premises with three inmates. Of course, she hadn't a penny so that's where I stepped up. Don't breathe a word to the Mrs…' He gets out his duster and this time mops his forehead.

'And all because she went after a man from a different race? That's very cruel?' Selma is on the edge of the easy chair and grasping her hands tight around me.

'None of those Planters—wanted to leave. They had an easy life in a manner of speaking. Out of indebtedness to Faultless for selling me the business well ahead of the British exodus, I let this poor thing come during the hot season. Each year Arleen says no, not that parasite and each year she eventually gives in. What to do?'

'She's got such a heart of gold... that woman of yours!'

'It's a diabolical business! Very cold-hearted. When they found out she was in the looney bin they went silent'

'Is it as bad as they say—in those places?' Selma asks with a frightened look.

'Worse! And all types... some are starkers jabbering to themselves... Sad that human beings can end up like that.'

'You'll get your blessing in heaven. Far better than running off to church -.'

My mother drops her voice as if afraid Arleen might hear. She may have noticed the distant rumble of the estate wagon at the bottom of the hill.
When Selma tucks me under the mosquito net in the guest room, I go to sleep thinking about the little girl Chappie was describing. That can't be the Virago in the annex? The Basket Case?

She looks like that small blonde princess with a
smocked frock in the poster of the Queen of England.
She wanders into a chilly dormitory looking for her
Mummy. As she tip-toes through, the dorm turns into a
carriage of a train.
There are lots of English ladies but they don't look
enough like the English Queen to be her Mum. The
ladies natter to each other,
...too young to be sent away
Quite heartless, don't you think?
Dear little Poppet..... so awfully young to be without
her Mamma?

The Elephant Pera-Hera has always been the highlight
of our stay. Acrobats cracking whips outside the
Temple of the Tooth, one hundred elephants dressed in
jewelled robes dotted with coloured fairy lights, tom-
toms and wailing conch-shell blowers, devil-dancers
from every corner of the island in lurid painted masks,
was the big finale to our holidays at the tea Estate. And
a feast of fireworks! But this year Arleen gets cold feet.

'It's a pagan thing. Pastor says sinful to partake
in pagan ceremonies,' she pouts over breakfast, which
is a pile of crispy rice flour cakes with a poached egg
nestling in the centre of each.

Everyone speaks together.

'What gibberish is this?' Chappie comes out of
hiding behind *The Ceylon Observer*.

'Ma, you promised you'd take us!'

'But Arl... we're only going to watch dear, not
going to partake!' Selma adds.

'What does Pagan mean, Ma?'

Arleen won't look up from her egg-hopper, which she breaks into tiny pieces for the birds. The chattering bunch called the Seven Sisters land on the veranda at the same time each day: these little birds come in sevens. They jabber busily as if buying vegetables in the market.

After their bird-gossip, they dart away. I love watching them chat in such a human way, listening to each other and nodding. I approach Arleen's chair holding my hand out for the bits.

She's so stroppy this morning she looks like a sulky hippo; her jaw square and sullen. Aunty Arleen lurches to embrace me but I side-step and take the bird food to where the Seven Sisters are gathering.

'Yes, this Pera-Hera festival—has been around far longer than-' Chappie scrapes his chair back to exit for morning Muster at the Factory ' anything going on in that American chapel! When we had Kandyan Royalty the King himself used to ride on the Temple Tusker. It's far older than Changing the Guard at Buckingham Palace, if you want to know!'

'What harm is there in watching some elephants and tom-toms?' coaxes Selma.

Arleen belches loudly and gives her husband a look to kill. He hurries off without looking back and forgets to grab his Solar Topee off the hat stand. The boys remain silent, not daring to argue now Pa has gone.

The night before our epic outing I get a fever and keep everyone awake with my cough. Aunty Arleen's honey bun gets doused with holy balm from Lourdes, bitter brown lung-tonic from the Ayurvedic dispensary and worst of all, inhalations with something the devil must have invented—Friars Balsam. I stink like a skunk so they move me into a small back room nearer the cookhouse where the small, crooked Umma sleeps on a thin floormat. It is a bare, little-used room with a stone floor and naked light bulb. Its simplicity reminds me of our train journeys.

Honiton is sorry to see me left out of the fun of the elephant festival. He dutifully piles his old comics on the rickety bedside table and asks if I'll be alright on my own? His Ma says if I need anything, to shout loud for Umma, because the old woman has lost her hearing. Honiton puts me through a rehearsal making me call out while standing the other side of the door, pretending he can't hear me.

'More than that! That Umma is deaf like a lamp post, I told you, no? Ah, you see that Soapberry tree out there? Look - It's the one where the fireflies live? It's like a light-show, no? That you can watch till you fall sleep'

The house sinks into quiet after Umma bashfully peeps at me before to say *Goodniee.* Her single word of English.

Feeling feverish, I doze in fits and sometimes wake to hear a woman's voice singing from the outdoor bathhouse. It must have been a dream because no one is home except Umma and me. Each time I wake from a doze, I want to cross over and put the light switch off, but the floor is so cold it puts me off making the short journey between door and bed. Outside the small window, fire-flies flit at the Soapberry tree and wink like tiny moving jewels from the Ratnapura river.

A hiss wakes me. It is so close that I look under my pillow.

'Sssssss!' it comes again, this time from under the bed.

I reach to gather up the bed clothes sufficiently to peep under the side of the iron bed. A second hiss comes from much closer. I move on knees to the foot of the bed without rattling it too much.

A cobra is coiled into an eight shape with its head upright only a few feet from me. The eyes hypnotise me. The sliver of a tongue is darting in and out. One side of my body goes numb with fear. I can't move.

I open my mouth to call out. No sound escapes my throat.

The snake is investigating the far end of the bed sheet now. In the distance heavy footsteps advance from the outside bath house. In panic I have forgotten the servant's name. I shut my eyes and a strangled sob escapes me. The footsteps halt. I take a breath and call out again, my eyes screwed against the sight of the slithering snake.

'Maaa…' my voice sounds far away, even to me.

175

The door creaks open. Basket Case woman peeps in, sees the snake and moves fast. She whips off a wooden clog and smashes it against the head of the cobra. Within seconds she is running out again. I curl up into a ball on the pillow, grabbing it to my chest for all it was worth. She is back. I am able to breathe again. She has her big spade with her. She is scraping up the remainder of the snake with it and the noise wakes the old servant who comes in rubbing her eyes and gathering her torn reddha around her.

Umma glares suspiciously at the large white woman, then runs outside without reaching me. All I can do is lay back and stare at the scene. Everything is blurry. I continue to stare. She is saying soothing words, though it sounds like a foreign language. I gawp back limply. My heart is buried under a sack of cement. I only hear thumping in my eardrums. Oh? She wants me to tell her something?

She looks ordinary in the dim electric light but seems awkward talking to children.

'Would you like me to… wait with you? Till they come home?' she asks gently.

I shake my head without thinking. I want to go back to sleep and wake up and find it was only a bad dream. I want my mother to get back and hug me. Minutes pass that feel like hours.

'I don't suppose you see many snakes where you live…' she is saying

I shake my head again….

'On tea-estates like this, cobras and bandicoots and porcupine are just ordinary creatures… but rather shy...'

Only my teeth chatter.

'When I left here to go on a big ship, to England… I was afraid too...'

'We… wa-was there cobra's there?'

'Oh no. None. I was terrified all the same. I had not seen snow before, you see?'

'Aaah?

'My mummy was not there…'

She was alone too…? She really does not look scary in this light…

'… and they had forgotten to explain that cold countries had snow. I thought that the snow would come to eat me…' She's smiling to herself.

My heart is bursting and I only hear its thumping. I can't reply. Then she is scooping up something into a gunny sack. I stare through the window to look for fireflies while the scrape of the spade against the cement floor keeps me from drifting off. I wait for the cobra's hiss but it does not come. The door is being shut. I hear her footsteps take her down the corridor. The light is still on. A car door bangs.

Umma's voice in the distance is shrieking 'Noona, enne noona!'

Voices in the distance get closer into the house. When I recognise my mother's laugh, I yell. I scream long after she reaches me, long after Arleen is holding me in her big floppy arms. I can't speak to tell them anything. All they make out of my jabbering is cobra… cobra woman…

Someone carries me to the big bedroom and everyone is speaking to each other but not to me. Umma is called in. Her answers are one long wailing which get shriller and shriller. I can't understand what she says.

'Did she do it darling? Was it the lady in the annex?' Arleen is getting agitated

I nod.

'Or did you have bad dream? Was it only a nightmare?' Selma clutches me tight.

'Not a nightmare… the cobra was hissing….'

'Did she come to your room, blossom?' Arleen's face is like an angry rhino, her eyes are mere slits and the abscess has returned to her cheek.

I nod. The events are beginning to roll back in my mind

'Umma was sleeping… she couldn't hear -'

Arleen stands triumphantly.

'See what I mean? I knew it… waited till the servant was out of the way.' She walks quickly out of the room, leaving me to my mother's comforting sounds. Selma drapes her shawl around my shoulders and strokes my head.

'She came… saved me!' I manage to mutter before dissolving into another bout of sobs.

Selma has let the veil of netting down to keep the insects away. I quite liked staring at the firefly tree from that small room. I don't see them now.

The boys run in excitedly.

'Where's Ma? Where's Ma? We found her burying the gunnysack in the back. Where's Ma?'

Out in the hallway, Arleen has misplaced her heart of gold. She exchanges harsh words with Chappie.

'Come and see for yourself! Burying the evidence…. we should have sent her packing when I found her bringing back the devil's brew from the Tavern.'

Selma tucks me tightly into bed and gives me her pillow smelling of cologne to cuddle. She is getting changed to join me in bed. The tent of netting separates me from the fury and excitement in the hall. I fall into an exhausted sleep, my sobs dry and only echoes of what had been.

The household is tucking into a breakfast of string hoppers and seeni sambol when I trail to the dining room in search of my mother. She is the only one eating with cutlery, the others are feasting with their fingers.

'Aaah, here's my baby at last! Come darling,' Arleen calls, hastily dipping one hand in the finger bowl and rubbing it against the table napkin. She has returned to her Heart-of-gold Arleen and envelopes me in her left arm as she calls out to the kitchen. I understand the word *Indiappa*. It feels like days since I've eaten.

'Give your aunty Arleen a good morning kiss, Cheruby! How's my sweet angel this morning?' she doesn't sound the same.

I think she's still angry with someone. I don't know what to say.

'Got such a nasty shock, didn't you my darling heart?' She spews kisses and I feel she may forget and gobble me up. Her breath wafts the pungent sambol, making my eyes tear. Her armpits smell of coal tar soap.

A plate of steaming hot *Indiappa* rice cakes arrives. Arleen doles out some on my plate, indicating I sit beside her.

Everyone at the table acts as if they have not seen me for months. Even Selma has a strained smile, like she does not expect me to know she's my mother. I am dying to tell them how brave cobra woman had been. How she killed the cobra with her spade; how she came to my rescue when my voice refused to work and knocked it senseless with her clogs. But I sit tongue-tied at the sight of their odd faces.

After some mouthfuls of *Indiappa*, I feel stronger and try out my voice.

'Where's … cobra woman?'

The boys look at Arleen and no one speaks. Then they look back blank as if they have turned deaf overnight. Arleen drags her chair around the corner and I feel another of her cuddle's coming. But she faces me squarely and takes both my bare feet in her hands and rubs them to make them warm.

'Don't think about that any more, my darling. That woman has gone. She won't be allowed to upset you again. No more cobras in this house You are quite safe, baby doll. We are not going to leave you alone anymore. That's a promise from Aunty Arl!'

I scoop up another rice noodle cake, dip it in the puddle of coconut hodi and stuff it into my mouth. It is warm and satisfying and reminds me how hungry I am.

'When does she get back?'

I'm sad I did not see her to say thank you for saving me.

With her mouth full of *Indiappa* Arleen burbles something incomprehensible. I look to Selma for translation. The tea in my mug is far too hot.

'Oh she's gone — back to where she belongs…' Selma seems upset too.

Why does nobody ask me about the cobra last night? Honiton looks down at his plate and belts up an envious smile. They got to the festival for elephants, drums and crowds of dancers. But all on my own I had a scary adventure. And I made friends with the one they were scared of! Wait till they know that…?

Arleen takes a deep breath.

'I don't know where she's gone to, sweetest, but I hope—for what she's done—that she ends up in the hottest part of hell! That's the place for that bleedy foreign maniac.'

GROUND CONTROL

Welcome to Xanadu! You must be Mr and Mrs
Lovelady - our honeymooners?

I am Henrietta, the Manager. Call me Hen.
Everyone does.

Seems like you've got here in a perfect slot to
have the infinity pool to yourselves… for a whole hour!
Now that is clever timing. And how was that long
stretch from the airport?

God, tell me about it! Fortunately, you were in
the capable hands of our splendid Jagarth. He knows
the clever routes on this island. I'll vouch he's erased
quite a few kilometres off your journey.

We have a cool drink for you, Jagarth—do go
and claim it?

So, shall I take you straight to your room? When
you've had time to recover, I can show you round the
old place. How's that?

You're going to ask me about tipping the driver. When you keep Jagarth for the whole stay you settle when you depart.

By then you'll know if he's earned his keep. If he is only dropping you off tip him, say—a thousand rupees per day.

About a Fiver. When they drag you round jeweller shops, Spice Gardens and whatnot they get rewarded by the merchants—even if you *didn't* buy that Sapphire! So pare down the baksheesh accordingly.

Ah, here's Dinesh with your Welcome Drinks— this stuff is nature's best remedy after a long flight. King Coconut—from the Xanadu estate, picked before sunrise. The Ayurvedic's won't drink coconut water after midday. I can't tell you why exactly but whatever time you swig it, it is the best cure for a hangover. I prefer mine with a tiny tot of Arrack. If you'd like to follow me through Mrs Lovelady. Ah there we are… just through… so this is your Imperial Peacock Suite!

Our rooms are named after the butterflies in this garden, thus Scarlet Turban, Black Raja and so on. I far prefer this room to our Honeymoon Suite because it overlooks the paddy fields. It's also the only room into which our Abeysinghe-family, Ebony four-poster can fit! You'll be excused for thinking you need a ladder to climb onto it. Lucky that you're both agile.

Oh? thank you—you noticed? Yes, the bed covers were my first bit of interior décor here. Indeed, yes, you're spot on! I used a Kashmiri wedding saree with genuine thread-of-silver woven in. Now this wooden veranda here is all part of your domain so if you choose, you may have breakfast in complete privacy. How about this—look… your own Buddha statue, if you feel the need to pray for rain!

Stunning, don't you think? I must say, I find paddy fields are meditation on a stick. It's hard to stop staring into them. Oh yes—your Safe for valuables – which I recommend you keep locked, hides inside this vast Portuguese *almirah*.

You can sublet that space out on its own, what? When it's turn-down time your steward will release the mosquito-nets over the bed. Among the Bath unguents we have made for us by a Slovenian herbalist who lives in the South, is a mosi-repellent made of Cinnamon oil, Pennyworth and Basil. Does the trick like nothing else! Pennyworth grows like a weed, she says, and they don't have a use for it. She's showing them alright.

Just remember, anything goes at Xanadu! Absolutely anything. As long as our guests are comfortable, that is what matters. Barefoot is the house style. Certainly, while there's no one around, what you wear in the pool is your affair. This folder has bumph about the area: try to fit in the three-temple walk at sundown. It's led by Bandula, the only one of our boys born in this village. He knows every crevice—his father was the Aristo's family gardener before him. Can't speak a word of English so he won't chatter! You will tiptoe through rice paddies. The quiet is nothing you've known; you see women in white sarees gathering for the evening Puja with baskets of lotus blossom—utterly off the tourist beat.

Well, it's back to the grindstone for lil' ole *moi*. I shall leave you to wind down, my dears. You can find me in my office off the courtyard when you feel in the mood for your tour. Okay?

A toodle oo!

And this dark cellar is where I slave and sweat and tear my roots out.

*When Travel Agents turn up to hound me for
their freebie 'Fam-Tours' we must remember to say The
Office! The book keeper and I call it Hell Hole.... sure,
it's had its slick of Titanium like the rest of the place
after its costly restoration.*

*That won't wash away the grisly dramas this ancient
Manor has endured. The Sinhala kings had a knack of
out-doing one another with the ghastliest tortures in
history. The least awful was being walled up alive.
These days they don't bother with bricks and mortar. A
thin wash of Titanium is all that's required.*

*If I had heard half the stories before starting
this job, I'd have legged it to Berwick St. Leonard's in
bare feet.*

*First things first, our Major Tom is nothing
whatsoever to do with the Military. Not a thing! Even
though it's happening miles from here, this horrible
war is still killing innocent civilians on the island. So, I
want that out of the way. No, our Major Tom is an
English entrepreneur living in Kuala Lumpur (quite
safe from the local Hu-ha!) Tells the world he is in the
Banking business! It has to be some business
processing money to afford this joint. The nickname
stuck when I emailed his weekly report saying Ground
Control to Major Tom! He chuckled about that
moniker: since then, he's been Major Tom. I've become
Ground Control.*

*Backstory. So, three months after starting this
costly project, Major Tom sadly lost his wife. Yes, poor
man, turning a hotel out of the manor house built by
our Kandyan Kings' Chief Minister was not his
priority, we can assume. In England we'd call it a
stately home; this Walauwa is a castellated Manor
house.*

After one single interview lasting from 6pm till breakfast the following day 'Major Tom' offered me this job. With no warning, certainly no previous training, I was installed as chatelaine of this ancestral Walauwa with 27 minions in designer sarongs.

You see I'd become a suddenly homeless gal when my Shirley Valentine episode went pear-shaped because Billi-the-Liar disappeared with my life savings. Well— one doth not waste time quibbling—I was up for virtually anything legal.

Our Steward's limited vocab was speedily enhanced, courtesy of the local British Council. They design a cunning conversation course just for waiters so the cretins wouldn't have a word of useful lingo – if they were to flit half way to become a Tuk-tuk driver. (They frequently do the nifty fuckers!) Old British Council know where their bread is buttered all right…. I was a tad anxious about leaping into something like this, damn right. Yet as someone said: God prevent me from a real job. It does so interfere with your day….

'You can do this standing on your head, you know that?' Vari assured me in her smoky voice 'The big advantage, my love… is, he can't be there to breathe down your neck. This poor-rich bugger has 6-year-old twins to mother and father, God help him… and I'm always here if there's anything you can't figure out. Stai tranquillo, Bambina!'

Vari is one of my Angels. She is known as Queen Bee of her own eclectic establishment overlooking the lake. It's a curious spot where rock stars fetch up if The Cure has got a bit tedious.

*Major Tom and stunned-little-Moi exchanged
the briefest of contracts. In the briefest of briefs, don't
you know? I was relieved to be rescued into lush
surroundings while miles from home. He was grateful
to a fool such as I, to take this burden on my shoulders.
The magic words 'paid flight home each year' did help.
A nifty Vari touch! Expert in negotiation. I could have
done with a wise owl like her in my Cinecitta days.
Magari! as our Italian friends say, If only!*

*She would have made gnocchi out of those
schifono!*

*You see these Areca nut palms —past the
bamboo grove—well they somehow grow thinner in
girth as they increase in age. Isn't it too wonderful?
Their trunks simply shrink; yes, you can read the age of
an Areca nut tree by its narrowing trunk—if not waist.
This estate is dotted—au-naturel—with many slim-Jim
palms. Satisfying to get slender as age takes one by the
hand, no?*

*A nasty blot on our idyllic landscape is, that
during The Uprising, our handsome eighteenth century
Walauwa—then the Abeysinghe Family Seat—got
invaded by militants. I'm not going to spoil your
appetite with torrid details, heavens no. Though one
incident I gleaned from Sarath, our garden designer did
give me one heck of a shudder.*
*We were sinking a glass of iced-tea in the Heliconia
plantation, when he pointed out twenty Areca nut trees,
he said he'd 'replaced' surrounding our infinity pool.
Hold on, I thought, getting curious.*

*'Replaced, you say—how d'you mean? Surely
these trees grew right here, Mr Sarath?'*
*Our diminutive gent mopped his forehead with his batik
kerchief, lowering his voice.*

'You see Madame, ow-er village gleaned a reputation during the terrible times due to er-hmn… some very awful killings which – did you never wonder, Madam – why not even one of your staff has been enlisted from this vicinity. Mmmnn… Understand?'

'Ah-oh? ...no, I don't think that I do?' My mouth gaping wide enough to catch a gecko. (You won't hear about that sort of detail in Lonely Planet.)

'Nobody from close villages will come anywhere near, certainly not lay their heads to sleep in this house—this Walauwa Abeysinghe—since the events of 1983. Even the high and mighty Abeysinghe clan were not safe. It was happening to big landowners all around the island. This part never gets lodged in history books. You see: they slaughter first, ask questions later…' His voice dropped to a hoarse whisper.

'Oh god! So, is this what they called… the Uprising?'

'Huh? No, no, no. Much later they thought up that word… to make it seem a people's revolution, against rich capitalists.' He stared at his feet, then the words tumbled out.

'Now what trees do those villains use to mount the heads of the poor victims? Areca nut trees, dear lady… Indeed yes, all the way from this drive of yours as far as the village. Oh, my heaven's me, such horrors took place that nobody will be coming to live on this side of our river for another twenty years. And hereby, how your English boss is getting this ancient palace for — only chickpeas!'

Crikey!

I did have a complete sense-of-humour-failure.

I needed to swallow something hefty when Sarath finally left me with his harvest of seven-foot Heliconia. We had the Bihai Claw that week.

I gradually returned to earth. Then the penny dropped: why my friends had been so alarmed on my behalf when I was hired so swiftly by the Expat hotelier. Vari, at the start had insisted in her strict voice,

'You must promise me pet: If ever, if ever there is the faintest whiff of trouble you will get the hell out of there, pronto?'

She was no scaremonger. A real pal. One can have a lark with any low perpetrator, but you do need your countrymen at times like these. She was looking out for me. She understood my conundrum. I had to turn this place around—heavy on scandal, light on electric wiring—in less than a month. And I had not even found a chef!

If the worst happened, the guests would have to darn well have to eat Curries, which even our garden boys can turn out blindfold, Allah-be-praised! If it had been my shout, d'you know, I would have let our guests experience all the local delicacies, but Major Tom is crippled by his Essex-boy-goes-grand idea. What's wrong with Mangoes, with Mangosteens, Tiger prawns, Negombo crab, that ultimate nectar—Murunga drumsticks in coconut broth? This yard-long, wild asparagus is heaven-sent! The adventurous grockles may bring themselves to try a soupcon of Durian—in a mousse presented on a fragrant Betel leaf? Now wouldn't that be heaven on a sunbed?

Oh no. Silly sod would not consider anything so authentic: he panders after 'boutique hotel nosh'. The words alone are like fingernails scraped on plaster. It's only a friggin' job, I keep repeating. Why do I allow myself to care? Ooh, honeymooners are approaching. All shush!

Well done, you two! You've spotted where I hide? Ha-ha!

Ready for a little tour, now you've recovered from that marathon drive? I must say, this getting married saga can be a tiring game. Far too much organisation these days, don't you think? One longs for the days of Gretna Green, know what I mean? I better show you to our infinity pool. I gather you will be a frequent flyer to it even before the birds awake, am I right? No, you won't disturb a soul! Even at six in the morning this water is a heavenly balm. I shall ask the pool boy to leave you to your training laps in peace.

So, tell me…. what age did you begin this punishing discipline? Whaat? Training to be a Pro at twelve… really? That's a supreme feat. So even on your honeymoon - you are telling me - no late nights, no alcohol, no smoking? Oh, my dear thing, you are a marvel? Like being a ballerina, what! I am in utter awe of people like you. I had a niece at Covent Garden; you must be one dedicated lady! I admire your stamina. Mental stamina, of course.

Now mind your heads under these arches— this is our Butterfly Bar. We should call it Butterfly Stroke in honour of you, ha-ha…? Originally, these were the cellars of the building. Mind you, they didn't keep wine in their cellars, more for provisions in the rainy season. And weapons too—I'm told they unearthed a considerable stash of priceless objects the builders chucked onto a bonfire heap. I kid you not! That was before my time, and it might have all been ashes if not that a bright architecture student photographing the restoration salvaged them - just in time.

Yes, I was thinking to mount the daggers and decorative swords over these main doorways. They might even come in handy to fend off trouble… in case a tribe of demons start their silly buggers again?

Just watch your step down this bit… You see the hills over that valley you can make out in the mist, Mr Lovelady? They are known as The Knuckles Mountains - on account of the four bumps. Four knuckles, d'you see? Now that's a great destination for athletic types. Magnificent waterfalls you may want to commune with, astonishing wildlife—Pangolin, Bears, even those elusive Leopards! Climbing Adam's Peak for sunrise is a once-in-a-lifetime experience. Herman Hesse wrote about his pilgrimage up that very Peak in *Siddhartha*. He returned to the island for a second attempt. You can borrow the book from our tiny library at the top of the stairs. You can't depart this earthly paradise without the supreme experience of Adams Peak!

Yes, cute as Jam Tree fruit and so deliciously in love!
I know… I'm a wretch for not warning the Lovelady poppets about our monk's horrendous 4 a.m. chant through those vile loudspeakers. Should I be offering my secret stash of earplugs, I wonder? Bit of a dampener, no? Having one's ears plugged on honeymoon? And why? A marauding horde of jungle-jimmies can materialise with firewood axes to lop off Areca nut palms or possibly… heads? I know how these worms can turn, in a jiffy. They simply do not possess a logic button. What. So. Ever! I had a very close shave with Billi-the-Liar. At least I was not present when he expired. So now I say, ask no questions and I tell no lies. Life is simply shorter in the tropics.

It's one of the facts of life here. It could so easily have been me they buried...?

Ta-daaaaaaa!

So, how's that as a sight for sore eyes my dear ones?

Your infinity pool, surrounded by paradise!

I keep the best for the last, as you can see. Mmnn…Heaven can wait, you might agree? Yes, all yours to enjoy…

The crickets will start serenading in a wee while. No actually, we had to install this pool, though the Walauwa has been here for two hundred years and there was a manor on the site for a lot longer, yes… I'm so glad that it's to your liking. You can understand why most of our clientele are honeymooners? It's everybody's dream destination.

I shall be on hand for another hour. Then Priti, our Aide-de-camp will cover for me in the hell-h… um, the Office. You may have noticed your complimentary Champagne in the room? Silva, your steward will be happy to chill and bring it to you here, if you prefer?

So my dears, if you think you have all you need…. I shall leave you to relish this velvety evening…? My great pleasure!

Have a splendid stay at Xanadu Mr and Mrs Lovelady.

And a perfect goodnight to you!

WRONG PARTING

I not remembering first time Mama go Middle East to work and leave Akki and myself staying with relatives. Maybe seven - I am that time, no? Only thing sticking in my head is faraway memory of one person angry as hell when I wet the bed. Even now I trembling when remember sleeping in wet sheet all night long because I scared to get smacking.

Second time Mama go to work Saudi stay in my mind like yesterday.

We sent to Mama's cousin's half-sister: we not know this family. Vivian Aunty have old fashioned house with wooden floor sounding like a stage. She putting dance music when time to give class. Nice dancing the ladies did, *aney,* I jealous I not join with them. Salsa dancing. And the shoes! I love high-heeled shoes they wearing. Two ladies in saree coming, must be sisters. One wearing red wedge-heels with purple flower size of my face. Other one has sequin shoes like beauty queens. Don't know what slaps husbands letting them have for gallivanting like that.

The dance class is why Akki like Viv Aunty's place, although box-room we sleep in, piled with suitcases this high! Above the door- which must stay open - otherwise can't even breathe, is small statue of Virgin Mary. Behind on glass panel someone has painted like a blue sky with tiny gold stars. So if cars passing outside it light up stars and give Holy Mother a sweet smile like she singing lullaby for make us sleeping. Making me think of Mama millions of miles far under sky with twinkling stars.

Virgin Mother keeping her also safe so she can save money and come. I try not to wet the bed here. Me am sensible girl by this time. I not want make anyone angry, but both Akki and I missing our Mama like nobody's business.

This is the time when Akki start crying in her sleep; so I having to get out from bed and stand in the dark, holding my big-sister hand. Me, the nangi!

'Don't cry, Akki. Mama will come... she bringing one gold bangle for you and one for me. She promise, no?'

I saying this over and over as if I am big one, if you please. Holy Mother keep smiling at me so I not afraid of dark. I can't tell if Akki hear me through her bad dreams but it stopping her sob her heart like a small *nangi*. I never having courage to tell my Akki she night-time crying because in the day, Akki being proper big sister. She plaiting my hair after combing the knots, make sure I am dressed ready for neighbour who taking us half way to school; scolding me good and proper if I forget to brush teeth with that peppery grey tooth powder this family is using, why I don't know? Even though Mama send us with two tubes of Kollinoss nothing toothpaste left in no time flat. Don't know who is taking?

Akki is Class Prefect. The organiser. Viv Aunty saying I am the dreamer.

Pretty as a picture with nothing between the ears.

I know what Vivian Aunty meaning. I understand!

That we so poor we haven't enough gold to make earrings.

Next-day-morning, as if Mama standing here listening to us talk, *patas,* she send letter to tell she bringing gold earrings for us! Yes! Every time she getting salary Mama going to Gold Souk to buy bangles before Ramadan holidays. *Aney!* that's how kind our Mama is. Working, working so hard. Otherwise, nobody will marry girls without gold on their arms, no?

This rich family Mama working for, not wanting her remain during Ramadan unless she agreeing fasting for one whole month! How they expecting Mama to fast when she's a Catholic? Because this problem we getting our Mama back for one month at Ramadan. This only time Akki stop crying in night time. Is better than Christmas when Mama staying. She bringing for us another set of gold bangles and matching dresses with tiny pin-tucks in yellow and pink. Strangers stopping in the road to ask if Akki and I is twins, even though Akki's hair is short as boy.

Her hair shining so much while Mama here to brush every day it looking like a crow's wing—purplish black. Coming to end of Mama's holiday, we ready to go back to Viv Aunty's house with Mother Mary statue to guard us. We not knowing that day before, our Dada—a drunk and wastrel— have cause havoc in middle of Viv Aunty's dance class, *Aney!*

He shouting he want his daughters back, yelling top of his head like a *goncase* then someone bringing policeman. When Mama taking us next-day-morning, *patas!* We not allow to stay anymore. I so sad for my Akki; she loving that music. I'm sad also that Viv Aunty can't see we have gold earrings now.

I like show her we have something between the ears.

Evelyn Nursery is a place calling after the widow who starting this Home for Girls. Mrs Samuel is old lady, ah, but Evelyn Home is respectable place for girls who have mother going far countries to work like nursing assistants and housekeepers. The day Mama bring us here I am learning hopscotch with the new children. Then Mama calling me inside to show how make shower to work. She un-pack and put our things in lockers beside the small iron beds. Mama explaining that because this Matron only speaking Sinhala, Akki and me not allow talk English anymore, liking or lumping. Even to each other? Not fair, no? Rules, it seems. Mama's eyes red like tomatoes when she leaving us because we now can't expect her telephoning every month. Phone calls not allowed. Matron say children complain and make trouble, telling for lies, food is tasteless!

Aney, that term taking long time to pass, never-ending. At Christmas time Hindu, Buddhist, Muslim girls all going holiday; only we Catholics at Evelyn Nursery without anywhere to go, what to do? Our Grandmother come and take to her house. We don't know this *Archi-Umma* very much so we shy to go with her. She talking Sinhala only. The day after Christmas at last we can speak to our Mama. She asking if we get presents, she sending? Did we go to Mass, Mama ask: did we miss her?

Then I cry and cry and can't speak anymore. Akki take the telephone and hug it tightly but she can hardly talk. So much we want to say to our Mama, but my throat like having a padlock—can't speak, *aney!* Suddenly we not remember how to talk English anymore….

Archi-Umma sorry for us because we without Mama at Christmas. She old lady so only know cooking tasty breadfruit chips and sambal. When she plaiting my hair, she making the braids so loose they come out, *patas,* by lunchtime. No children to play, no relations, nothing doing. Mama has given for us a calendar to count the days before she returning. So, I don't get sad when *Archi-Umma* putting us to Evelyn Nursery three days before school starting.

I run to find my red crayon to tick the days on my calendar. After forever-an-ever the day arrive when our Mama returning. This time Mama coming in morning so we not sent to school. When other girls ready in school uniform, we wearing Sunday frocks and brand-new socks. Mama writing already, telling things she is bringing. She getting present for Archi-Umma also. We read this letter about twenty times! I smell our Mama on the paper of that letter. Smell her lovely shining hair.

Akki and I wake long time before the bell, excited, chatting this and that. Akki getting idea Mama is finish working in Middle East, now returning home for always. I can't think how she knowing this? Maybe she having a dream? I hoping she is right, *aney!* All my life I wishing Mama haven't got that job to go and leave us. Mama's airplane taking long-long time. Matron saying maybe plane broken? I am not thinking this. Planes cannot break, I don't think? At lunch interval we sent to the back-house to eat with Mrs Samuel. She very kind lady, not like matron!
Big girls saying she make favouration for Akki because she giving Fruit Pastilles to us when Sweetie Time. After we saying Grace, Mrs Samuel tell special prayer to Virgin Mary for Mama's safe journey.

Later other children returning from school and one by one, relatives take home. Each time new person coming Akki and I jumping and running with a big grin thinking our Mama. We know her suitcase will be size of Maradana Station! After every children leave and go, some tall girl coming, talking to matron. Akki not remembering her but say she look like one of our relations. She not wanting speak Akki or me; not interested to look even. Matron now in hurry to go holiday so giving this girl our *goma*-green suitcase and telling us that this one—her name we don't know—taking to show where is our Mama.

We getting tired now because waking up early. Hard to keep up with girl walking this way, that way, not say where she taking us. We wait long time in bus depot, very crowded. Lucky we are finding a seat together because in a tick, Akki starting cry now—even though soon-soon we see Mama.

When we struggling off bus, dizzy because very hot, this girl with nose like a *pittu bambua*, grab us and ask suddenly if we have eaten any food? Why she angry with us for no reason? She stopping outside a hospital kind of place and buying a lunch packet. Mama always telling never to eat on roadside. Never to eat without washing hand. We take lunch packet she giving and follow inside building where people giving funny look to us.

I try talking to my sister, 'Why Akki, what for, you not happy to see Mama?'

Akki just give me her water bottle to hold. She won't talk even, same as that day after Christmas when Mama telephoning to us.

After sitting on a hard bench another long time, that man in charge calling out our name. The tall girl name Miss Perera. Now at last we know. She having our birth certificate and showing the man. Man having face like that drunk man standing at railway station, he walking dark corridor with doors this way, that way. I can't think why Mama want us meet here? Still the tall girl nothing saying.

The man asking Akki what my age? And her age? He asking questions to Miss Perera but not listening answer. I certain she must be cousin because she having our papers, no? Why she not wanting talk? Then other whole time waiting, waiting, after we follow through another corridor.

Here is cooler. Air-conditioned like a hotel: very noisy the machinery rattling. The man taking us into dining hall place where the far-side wall having steel boxes. He checking something with the file.

Miss Perera fed up like she going to leave us and run as if house on fire. Man pulling handle of the steel box and a long drawer coming sliding out. Icy and misty inside so it taking time before I make out our Mama's face has changed since the last time. She so ragged and thin. Tired of being in this long drawer. Someone make big mistake! They putting our Mama's parting on wrong side of head, *aney!* She has no earrings, no necklace. Where her Saint Anthony medal gone - she every time wearing it?

Why Mama not in hospital bed, if so sick?

I staring at Akki to see what to do? My sister's face is squeezed into a scream but no noise coming. Akki is frozen in middle of her scream. I asking over and over, what is the matter with our Mama? Tell will you, what is matter Akki?

Miss Perera for first time speaking. She saying in angry voice

'What you think is the matter with her?'

I look at Akki - our lunch packet smashed on ground all over her feet, dirty floor, rice everywhere. *Aparade!* Such a wasting, no?

Now this Evelyn Nursery is Akki and my forever-home.

Before I falling to sleep in iron bed, that picture of Mama with that wrong parting flashing in my eyes over and over. I can't erase. How is possible our Mama have gone to live in heaven with angels and all, while her hair in that wrong parting? Shame *aney*!
Mama have always hair in such pretty style.

What the devil God will think, ah?

AUTHOR

Tania, a story teller from Sri Lanka, hit the Sixties streets running, while still a kid.

Rootless for most of her childhood, Tania was welcomed into 9 Listed Buildings in London and the Shires. She had a brief career in Italian Cinema, then interviewed celebrities for Penthouse, Saga, The Evening Standard and Apa Guide Publications.